# CONTENTS

THE FIERY CHARIOT

AN ARDALBA STORY

MÁIRE WELFORD

MERCIER PRESS

1

## Back to Ardalba

Brona and Róisín waited at the town hall in Glenelk and watched Rory and Aidan coming up the street to meet them. They had all been home for their dinners after school, and now they could do what they liked until teatime.

Glenelk looked lovely in the spring sunshine. From where they stood they could see the Seven Arch Bridge on their left, where it crossed the Whitewater river, and St Olaf's Church and their school straight ahead. All around them the street was full of life: Glenelk was always busy.

'Hurry up!' Brona called to the two boys. 'We've been waiting here for ages.'

Aidan and Rory ran up, full of excuses. 'We had jobs to do,' Rory panted. 'My mother wanted me to bring in stuff for the fire.'

'And mine wanted the dustbin washed out,' Aidan said. He was out of breath too.

'Well, you're here now,' said Róisín, 'so where do we want to go until teatime?'

No one said anything for a minute. Then, almost together, each of them suggested in a whisper, 'The Valley of Rocks?' They looked at each other and burst out laughing.

'I was afraid to mention it,' Brona said. 'I thought you'd

all want to keep away from there for ever.'

'The Valley of Rocks is one thing,' Rory pointed out, 'but do we want to go the whole way? Do we want to go back to Ardalba?'

No one answered that at once. Each of them remembered their time there. There had been hardship and danger, but it had been a wonderful adventure, like nothing else that had ever happened to them. But to go back . . . !

'We don't have to decide that right away.' Aidan sounded unsure. 'We can go as far as the inner cave anyway, and check that our clothes and rings are still safe.'

'Yes, let's do that,' Brona said decisively. 'We can decide later if we want to go further.'

It was nearly a month since they had walked by chance into the Kingdom of Ardalba. None of them had forgotten that when they left the fort of Maeve of the Thousand Spears, her guards and hunting dogs had been on their heels, trying to find and capture them. What would happen to them if they returned?

Now they followed Brona down the road past St Olaf's Church and their school, on out to the Valley of Rocks. When they got there, they stopped and looked at each other uncertainly.

'Come on,' Rory said at last. 'Stones won't harm us.'

They climbed down among the rocks, leaving green fields behind them, and walked along the desertlike valley filled with oddly shaped sandstone rocks. These rocks had been moulded over time by wind and rain into strange, awesome shapes that owed nothing to the skill of human hands. It was a bleak, desolate spot. Each of the four felt a shiver of excitement. The Valley of Rocks seemed menacingly silent; outside sounds became muted and distant. It was an alien landscape, like the mountains on the moon.

'Do we want to go into the caves?' Róisín said, giving everyone a chance to opt out. 'We don't have to.'

'Let's go in and check on the clothes anyway,' Aidan suggested. 'We need to know whether they've been disturbed, and whether our rings are still there.' They knew they could not return to Ardalba without the moonstone rings that marked them as high nobles at Maeve's court, and which enabled them to call on second sight in moments of danger.

This time they had no torch to show them the way. They pulled aside bushes that hid the entrance to the outer cave and stepped inside. Here there was plenty of light to guide them to where they could wriggle into the inner cave. Brona was first in. She helped the others squeeze their way through the narrow opening, until all four of them were inside.

In the inner cave, the light was dim, coming from the gap they had just wriggled through. It was enough to guide them to the corner where they had left the clothes they wore escaping from Ardalba: slaves' cloaks and tunics, worn over their own clothes. Would they now put them on again and return to Maeve's world?

'Look for the rings,' Aidan said. 'If they aren't there, we shouldn't go back.'

While they rummaged through their clothes, they recalled their previous experiences, remembering Scathach, the Black Bull of Wisdom, Samhain's crannóg and the time they had consulted the Stone all by themselves to save Samhain's life.

Each of them shook out their slave garments until they found the travelling sacks. Sure enough, the rings were where they had left them, hidden in these sacks.

'We've got everything,' Rory said. 'What do we do now?'

'No one here will miss us,' Róisín reminded them. 'When we leave this era, time stands still for us until we get back.'

'What about Ardalba time?' Brona asked. 'How much time

has passed there since we left a month ago? And what sort of trouble are we going to be in with Majesty?'

'When we left, the guards were still below us on the hill. No one saw us. They're probably not looking for us any more. In slave clothes, we could split up and wander about to see what's happening. Then we could decide whether to go on, or to come back here.' Rory's plan seemed sensible.

'That sounds OK to me,' Róisín said. 'We can't come to much harm if we're careful.'

'If that's what we're doing,' Brona said, 'why not change into slave clothes now and leave our Glenelk clothes here until we get back, instead of wearing them under our slave clothes?'

'That's all right as long as no one finds them before we get back here.' Aidan sounded uncertain.

'No one knows about the inner cave except us,' Rory reminded him. 'I don't think they know about the outer one either.'

'In any case, how *could* anyone find them?' Róisín asked. 'While we're in Ardalba, time here stands still. So no one would have had time to come into the cave and find our things, would they?'

In the end they agreed to change into their slave clothes before they went any further. After changing, they took a good look at each other to make sure nothing was out of place. They left their own clothes behind them in the cave, in tidy bundles.

'We're all set, then,' Róisín said at last. 'Let's go.'

Aidan went in the lead this time. The others followed, keeping one hand on the cave wall and the other on the person in front of them. They were in total darkness now, the kind of blackness you find only in caves. They knew from the last time that they could not get lost. There were turns in the passage, but no other passage opened out from it where they might wander off and miss their way.

Before long, they reached the second turn and knew they would soon see light ahead. Then they were at the cave opening, which was thickly covered with bushes.

'Last chance,' Aidan whispered. 'Do we all want to go on?'

Behind him he heard three whispers of 'Yes, we do.' Carefully he pulled aside the bushes, and one by one the children crept out into the open air.

# 2

## THE RETURN TO MAEVE'S FORT

'Look!' Rory pointed down the hill. 'The guards are exactly where we saw them when we left. Are they still looking for us, or for someone else?'

'Whoever they're looking for, they're right where they were before, because while we were back in Glenelk, time stood still here in Ardalba. It works both ways.' Aidan looked pleased about this. 'That means that when we do meet Maeve, we won't have to explain where we've been for the past four weeks, because she won't have missed us at all.'

'That is, if you're right and she hasn't missed us already.' Róisín sounded worried.

The four looked down at the men searching the lower hillside. They watched them shaking every bush, looking behind every rock. It would be hard to get past them and return to the palace unseen.

Just then, a bodhrán sounded its beat from the fort. It was a faster, more intermittent beat than they had ever heard before. It stopped for a few seconds and then began again, and went on stopping and starting.

'That's sending a message,' Aidan said, 'the way trumpets used to do.'

The children watched the searching men pause to listen

to the bodhrán. Then their leader called them together and they all began to go back to the stronghold.

'It called them back,' Rory said. 'They're on their way.'

'What do we do now?' Brona asked. 'Is this a good time to try to get to our rooms without being seen?'

'I think it is,' Róisín said. 'Whatever's going on, those guards will have to report to Maeve, and everybody will be in the great hall to find out what's happening. No one will miss us, or even think about us.'

'I agree,' Rory was still staring at the retreating guards. 'The sooner we get back, the better.'

Without further delay they set out separately for the fort, far behind the searchers, who would soon join the throng they could see assembling in front of the stockade. When the guards had melted into the crowd, the four got together again.

'No point in going back in ones and twos when no one at all is looking at us, is there?' Aidan asked. The others agreed, and they all scurried back together as fast as they could. They approached the fort far on one side, heading back to the tiny gate at the back by which they had left.

'Will we get to our rooms without someone challenging us?' Brona was concerned that someone would notice them in their slaves' clothes and wonder what they were up to.

'Who'll catch sight of us here when everybody is out at the front of the palace?' Rory asked. 'Didn't we see them all coming through the main entrance into the stockade? The passages will be empty. We'll have no trouble.' Rory seemed certain about this.

They went through the back gate and in through the palace's back entrance, which high nobles never used. From there, they hurried back to their rooms.

'Get your high-nobles clothes on as quickly as you can,'

Aidan advised. 'We need to join everyone out front before they begin to wonder where we are.'

In no time at all, they met again in the passage. Brona and Róisín were wearing soft linen dresses that reached to their ankles, held in place with jewelled belts and shoulder pins. They also wore cloaks of navy lined with violet and pink to match their dresses. Aidan and Rory were in knee-length tunics with ornamental belts, and in sandals with thongs up to the knee.

'I hope no one notices our hair,' Brona said. They had all done their best but had not been able to dress their hair as skilfully as their attendants usually did.

'Come on! Hurry!' Aidan raced in front of them towards the palace entrance.

They reached the back of the crowd but could not see what was happening, or why everyone was out there. Róisín saw her attendant, Áilne, among the throng and went over to talk to her.

'We slept,' Róisín said. 'What's been happening? Why the crowds? Is there an enemy?'

'No enemy, madam,' Áilne replied. 'Noble Dervla could not find her small daughter anywhere in the palace. We feared for her safety. Majesty sent out searchers, for fear she had been stolen away.'

'Did they find her?' Róisín guessed now why the guards had been recalled.

'Yes, madam. They found her sleeping beside a newborn calf in the animal enclosure. Dervla is bringing her back to her room.'

At that moment, the crowds in front of them parted. Maeve came through, leading Dervla, who carried her small daughter. The children could see Dervla had been crying, even though she was smiling now. They stood aside for the queen and Dervla. Behind them came Maeve's husband Ailill and their son Magdawna.

'Come inside with us,' Magdawna said to the children. 'You missed all the excitement.' They followed him into the great hall.

'We were asleep,' Aidan said. 'We just heard that searchers found Dervla's little girl unharmed.'

Soon everyone at the fort returned to what they would normally do at that time of day. The four children sat in one of the window seats, glad that they did not have to explain their absence to Maeve or anyone else.

Later, while attendants prepared the evening feast, everyone heard a horn sounding loudly outside the outer fence. Silence fell in the judgement hall. Maeve listened intently to the horn repeating its call. 'That is a herald from Datho,' she announced, and sent a messenger to bring the herald into her presence. He was a small man, who reminded Brona of a jockey, or someone who would be at home on a horse. Advancing, he bowed deeply to Maeve and her court. 'Welcome,' Maeve said in her firm, strong voice. 'I hope your master, Lord Datho, is well.'

'My master is well and sends you greetings, O Maeve of the Thousand Spears, wife of Ailill, King of the West, Keeper of the Moonstone, Guardian of the Black Bull of Wisdom, Great Ruler of Ardalba that stretches as far as Shining River.'

After this formal address, the messenger bowed deeply once more before delivering his message.

'My master sent me to issue his challenge to you to take part in a chariot race he has planned for the day after the next full moon. Lord Datho challenges all the kingdoms in our land and also Picts, Saxons and Celts from across the seas and from the islands. He has invited entrants from Man, the Outer Islands and the Northern Lands, as well as from our own islands west of your kingdom here, and those off the shores of his brother Cian's kingdom to the south.'

'Thank you, herald.' Maeve's tone was gracious. 'We accept Lord Datho's challenge. For what honour does he wish us to race?'

'Lord Datho recently commissioned his master silversmith, Samhain, to make him a unique silver bowl. It is worth a king's ransom. No one will ever match its workmanship, or produce a more beautiful design. This is the trophy he offers to the winner.'

Rory poked Brona and whispered, 'That's the bowl I rescued from the robbers who stole it from Samhain. It was nearly too heavy to carry.'

Brona nodded. None of them would ever forget that adventure.

'And where will Datho hold this race?' Maeve seemed to be full of interest in the contest.

'Majesty, competing chariots will run on the Plain of Mighty Stags, where Lord Datho has his fort. This seems fair to him, as he will not himself be competing for the prize. Even now he is preparing a mighty track, levelled and covered with sand, where chariots may group, and when it is time, where they may race.'

'Thank you again, herald, and my thanks to your master, Lord Datho. Pray tell him it will be our pleasure to take part in such a contest and, by winning the race, prove that Ardalba is second to none.' Maeve turned to her attendants, showing her usual kindness to travellers to her court. 'I would have you provide food for this weary man, and give him resting place,' she instructed them. The herald left the hall, and the queen looked around at her nobles. 'Here is a chance to defeat Lú publicly and damage his pride,' she said.

'I am your champion charioteer,' Magdawna said to his

mother. 'It is an honour for me to race under your standard.'

Maeve looked thoughtful, her violet eyes sparkling with anticipation. 'We must prepare well,' she said. 'We will not win this contest easily. Our proud white horses will meet their match. They must practise, and so must you, Magdawna. But what a chance it is! To snatch such a trophy from the very best teams among the islands, and from charioteers from foreign lands! The name of Maeve will be known far and wide. Lú will lose respect when my champion defeats him.'

Before the feast, everyone began to discuss the race, and when the feasting was over Maeve's harper sang loud praise of the queen's fighting spirit and her fabled white horses.

# 3

## MAEVE CONSULTS SCATHACH

The following morning Datho's messenger went on his way, and Maeve called together her council of state. As this included all her high nobles, the four children were present and would be heard equally with everyone else who had ideas to offer.

Maeve sat before her nobles, a queenly figure. She had plaited her red-gold hair with golden beads. Her ankle-length tunic of emerald linen was stiffly embroidered in gold and violet, setting off the colour of her deep-violet eyes. Golden clasps adorned the tunic and a golden belt held it at her waist. Over her gleaming hair she wore a golden band enriched with jewels, and at its centre shone her moonstone, echoing emerald glints from its misty depths.

'I have called you here to discuss Datho's challenge,' she said. 'You must all realise how important it is for us to win the trophy. We cannot lose prestige, or allow Lú to emerge as winner. It is a matter of pride in ourselves and our kingdom.'

The nobles agreed with this. They simply could not let Lú win. How to prevent him was the problem, though, because they all knew that he had magnificent horses and renowned charioteers, and that he would stop at nothing to defeat Maeve of the Thousand Spears. Neither could they allow the trophy to go to any foreign competitor. The shame of that could not be borne.

'The key is to train our horses until they are fit and fleet-footed.' This suggestion came from an older noble called Bran.

Another noble then spoke. 'We must also have our charioteer practise every move again and again, until he develops stamina, experience and lightning-fast reflexes.'

'The moon was full last night,' the queen reminded them all. 'We have no more than twenty-seven sunrises before it is full again. Can we practise enough in that time to be sure of victory?'

A beautiful courtier named Iseult spoke next. 'Majesty, she said, 'we must have spare teams of horses in case any horse goes lame, and although no charioteer could match your son, Magdawna, others should be trained and ready in case an accident befalls him.'

'I agree with that, Mother,' Magdawna said. 'The race must not depend on me alone or on one team of horses. I suggest having four teams in readiness. And others must train with me. As to time, if we start preparations at once I believe we can be ready.'

'That is the plan we shall follow.' Maeve spoke decisively. 'Now, as to horses . . . ' At once, many of her nobles volunteered their prize animals and sent slaves off to fetch them.

Brona spoke up. 'Majesty, Aidan and I both have experience riding horses, although we could scarcely match Magdawna's skill. May we volunteer to train the horses each day, before Magdawna practises for the race? We would soon have them working at their best.'

'You have served me well until now,' the queen replied. 'It pleases me to give the training of my racing teams to you.'

The council of state broke up after hearing Maeve's decision. Some went to sort out the four teams Magdawna had asked for. The children went back to Aidan's room to decide how best to organise the training of the horses. 'We will train and exercise Magdawna's team first, in the early morning,' Aidan said. 'We will build up the horses' speed, stamina and obedience. If we take them up the mountain path through the trees, it will increase their fitness.'

'What mountain path?' Rory asked.

'The wooded mountain behind the fort, up the gorge to where the waterfall is,' Aidan said. 'It's steep, but there's a path through the trees.'

'How do you know that?' Brona asked. 'We've never been up that mountain.'

'Our attendant, Bress, comes from beyond it,' Aidan said. 'It's called Boar Head Mountain. He has often described it. The path goes almost to the top.'

'It sounds like a wild place,' Róisín said. 'We should have it to ourselves.'

'So each morning we start up there with Magdawna's team, with each of us taking one of the four horses? Is that what we'll do?' Rory wanted to be quite sure about it.

'Yes,' Aidan said. 'Then, while they rest, we'll ride and train the second team. We'll instruct senior grooms to do the same somewhere else for the third and fourth teams. When Magdawna practises with the chariot and his own team, Brona and I will take turns to practise with and compete against him, using the second team, as we are more experienced riders than you and Róisín. Do you all agree to this?'

'Of course we do,' said Róisín. 'Don't we, Rory?'

'Yes, of course,' Rory said. 'I couldn't drive one of those racing chariots faster than walking pace.'

The children spent the rest of that day choosing horses

for the three teams from those offered by other high nobles and from Maeve's own stables, making sure that the best of them made up the second team. Then they went to make friends with Magdawna's horses and left everything ready for an early start the next day.

Their last task was to report back to Maeve where she sat among her nobles in the great hall, as she had the first day they had seen her. They bowed low before her. Aidan spoke for all of them. 'We can start training at first light,' he said, 'but Majesty, we alone cannot guarantee victory. Is there any aid you can give us?'

'I shall call Scathach, my arch-druidess,' Maeve offered. 'She cannot help me see the future, but I will be able to discover what Lú does in the present.'

This time, no bodhráns announced the arrival of Scathach. Before they knew it, she stood silently in the entrance. A tall wolfhound stood on either side of her, their rough coats in contrast with her magnificent druid's robes. Her midnight-blue cloak was silver-lined, its hood putting her face in shadow and covering her raven-black hair. Her right hand held her druid's staff, which was resting upright on the ground. Glowing emerald eyes in its snake's head threw out green sparks, which seemed to float above her in the air.

The room grew hushed as nobles became aware of her presence. When they had all become still, Scathach walked across the great hall to where Maeve stood, and bowed profoundly before her. 'You summoned me, Majesty,' she said. 'How can I use my power to help you?'

Maeve bowed in return to her druidess. The queen then explained to her about Datho's challenge, and her own fears that Lord Lú of the North might not play fair. 'We need to know what he does,' she said, 'and how he prepares himself for this challenge. I ask that you help me read the Stone.'

Scathach spoke with power and authority, her low-pitched voice reaching all corners of the hall. 'I am here to assist you in every way I can,' she said. 'Pray kneel, and we shall consult the Stone.'

The children watched Maeve kneel on a cushion offered by Ailill, her husband. Scathach approached her. She handed her staff to Magdawna before placing her hands on the shoulders of the queen. The wolfhounds sat on either side of her, their watchful eyes on the druidess. The moonstone in the centre of Maeve's tiara radiated from its milky depths sparks of blue, red and emerald green.

Scathach gazed intently at the Stone. She spoke to Maeve in soothing tones. 'In your mind, Majesty, you must see the Stone. Keep its image before you. Let all other thoughts go.' Maeve's eyes closed. Her breathing seemed to slow down. Scathach continued to speak. 'See the Stone, Majesty. Look deep into its cloudy depths. Watch the colours it reflects. Let other thoughts go.'

The children watched, knowing exactly what was happening. They remembered the day they had read the stone by themselves, to find Datho's silversmith, Samhain, when he was lost. They had never told anybody that they could do it, that they did not need help from Scathach or from the Black Bull. That was *their* secret.

Now Scathach was asking Maeve to tell them what the Stone revealed to her. 'What do you see, Majesty?' she asked. 'Can you see Lú? Speak now.'

Maeve responded in dreamy tones, her voice soft and halting. 'I see Lú in council,' she said. 'I see Archeld at his right hand, but I can hear nothing.' She paused, then continued, 'I see Lú and his anti-druid leave the council. They go outside the fort to where Lú's horses wait.' Maeve paused again, this time for longer.

Scathach spoke once more. 'What can you see now, Majesty?' she asked urgently. 'Tell us what you see.'

'I see fire.' Maeve's tone was puzzled. 'I see Archeld and Lú looking at fire. It is radiant. It is golden like the sun. I cannot see beyond its brightness to what it is. Now they leave the fire to return to the horses. Why do they laugh? Why do they look so pleased?' Her voice faded.

Scathach took her hands from the queen's shoulders, and removed her gaze from the moonstone. Maeve, still looking dazed, opened her eyes. Magdawna held out his hand to help her up from the ground.

'Fire!' Maeve said. She turned to Scathach. 'What does it mean?'

Scathach pondered briefly. 'There is obviously danger for us in fire,' she said. 'Be vigilant. Put guards to watch your horses. Bid your slaves take extra care when they handle fire. I cannot see clearly when the danger will strike or where it comes from. But Lú and Archeld are behind it. So beware!'

'Thank you, Scathach.' Maeve looked around her at her nobles. 'You have all heard the arch-druidess. Be watchful.' Then she gave Scathach leave to withdraw.

When Scathach was gone, Maeve spoke to the children. 'I am sorry I did not see more clearly what danger lies ahead,' she said. 'But I know you will be watchful.'

She had attendants bring Aidan and Brona the clothes of charioteers: short white tunics, and leather greaves to protect their shins.

Everyone left the great hall, and the four returned to their rooms.

'An early start tomorrow,' Aidan reminded them as they parted. 'We begin to train and exercise Magdawna's team at first light.'

# 4

## THE WILD HORSE OF THE MOUNTAIN

From then on, the four children spent all their time with the horses, exercising and training them. Magdawna's team of horses were his own beautiful thoroughbreds, the best in Maeve's stables. Each morning Aidan led this team to Boar Head Mountain, to build up their stamina on its steepest trails.

'These workouts should help them race faster than any horse trained on the plains,' Rory said, as he guided his mount up behind Brona's.

'They should,' Aidan agreed, 'but after three days, do any of you see them performing any better? We'll have to work them harder, and in the evenings race them harder. The second team will have to give them a tougher contest when we practise racing against Magdawna's horses.'

They continued up the gorge, deafened by the sound of water thundering down on their right from falls high above them. On their left trees stood thickly, their pale brown trunks bare, dense branches high above blocking the sunlight. Further and further up they took the horses, until at last they saw the waterfall like a bridal veil, a white torrent that gushed from rocks far above them before plunging to the distant river bed below. They followed the winding forest path until they passed above the waterfall, then they descended in its narrow gorge. The atmosphere of this eerie, gloomy, silent place affected them. The only sound apart from the thundering falls was the snorting of the horses and the slow clip-clop of their hooves.

'Let's get off and lead them for a while.' Rory watched feathery trails of mist – almost white in the gloom – blow from the horses' nostrils.

'Good idea,' Aidan agreed. 'A walk uphill will do us good too.'

Soon they reached a fork in the path; they were not sure which way to take. Trees stood around them like ghosts in the morning mist. Suddenly, without a sound, a mighty stallion appeared among them. His coat was as black as coal, his tail and mane creamy white. He blew plumes of golden flame from his nostrils, and diamond-white light sparked from his brown eyes. The stallion stood motionless until the four children and their horses had all become aware of his presence. Seeing him, the horses moved closer together and stood still.

'What a beauty!' Brona exclaimed.

'Four of *those* and there would be no contest in the chariot race,' Aidan agreed.

The stallion moved nearer with delicate steps, shaking his head and snorting quietly, until he stood directly in front of them. Brona, always fearless, approached with Róisín to rub his velvet brow. When they stood back from him, they heard him speak in husky grunts. He spoke human words directly to their ears instead of sending sounds into their minds as the Black Bull, King Elk and Badger had done.

'I am Pooka, Wild Horse of the Mountain. I can lend you my power in the race you will run. Your horses will learn from me, and no one will defeat them.'

'What must we do, noble Pooka?' Aidan asked.

'Bring your horses to me every day, but bring them secretly. I will help Maeve of the Thousand Spears, but I want no others to learn of my secret mountain paths.'

'Of course we'll tell no one,' Róisín assured him. 'We have been on secret missions before for Queen Maeve.'

'Had I not known that, and how you brought the Black Bull of Wisdom to safety, I would not offer my help now.'

Each of the four wondered how Pooka had found out about the bull. As if reading their thoughts, he said, 'King Elk visits all mountains in his kingdom, and recently he visited mine. That is how I learned of your brave journeys. Now, because Elk promised you protection in the animal world, I will protect you here, and help you prepare these horses for the contest.'

'Thank you, Pooka.' Rory spoke for them all. 'When the sun has risen twenty times more, we will leave with the horses for the Plain of Mighty Stags in Lord Datho's kingdom. They must be at their best by then. We really need your help.'

Pooka tossed his head at this. He stepped up to Magdawna's horses, facing each in turn. He softly breathed fire into their nostrils as they stood before him, then whinnied loudly, rearing up on his hind legs. 'Now, mount them,' he said to the children. 'You will ride them. I will lead them, and begin their training.'

Straightaway, the horses were full of energy, bounding up the forest path after Pooka. He took them along one path and then another, sometimes uphill, sometimes down. Brona could see the horses' muscles move under their gleaming white coats and could hear them breathing more easily than before.

Pooka came to a halt when he had brought them all back to the place where they had started. 'I will do that every day,' he said. 'Bring your second team to this same place today to meet me, and they too will grow in strength.'

'We'll bring them up now,' Róisín promised. 'Do you know if Lú and Archeld will be able to see us training here with you by looking through their precious ruby, the way we look through our moonstones?'

'My mountain is always under a cloak of invisibility,' Pooka said. 'You are safe here from Archeld's evil spells.'

'We are afraid of fire,' Róisín said. 'Maeve saw fire when she looked at Lú through the moonstone, and Scathach has warned us to be alert.'

'Then be on your guard,' Pooka said, 'but on my mountain you will always be safe.'

Aidan and Brona led Magdawna's team down Boar Head Mountain and back to Ardalba, where they could rest. Then they took the second team up to meet Pooka, who began the horses' first training session right away.

\*

Maeve's slaves had prepared a circuit on level ground where Magdawna could practise with his chariot, and where Aidan could compete with him. In late afternoon, everything was ready for their first practice race. The whole household came to see what chance Magdawna had in Datho's competition.

Magdawna brought his team to the starting point with a flourish. Then Aidan drove up in another of Maeve's war chariots, drawn by the second team, his white tunic gleaming, chestnut leather greaves shining on his shins. When the starter's flag was dropped, everyone gave a roar and the two chariots leapt forward. They were neck and neck for the first three laps, and then, in the fourth lap, Magdawna began to creep ahead. The race lasted ten circuits; by the end,

Magdawna was three lengths ahead of Aidan and claimed the victory.

Afterwards, Magdawna and the children made their way back to the fort. 'What training have you given my team?' the prince asked the four children. 'Never have they pulled so well together, nor shown such strength.'

'We're keeping that a secret for the time being,' Róisín replied. 'If they're that good today, after only four days of training, what will they be like for the race?'

After the evening feast, the children felt tired. They went back to their rooms for an early night, so as to be up and ready the next morning for another training session with Pooka, Wild Horse of the Mountain.

# 5

## MAGDAWNA PRACTISES

Every day, the children took the horses up Boar Head Mountain to meet Pooka, and each day, before leading their training, Pooka blew his spirit into Maeve's white chargers. The horses and children learned together how to take sharp bends at speed, how to move as a team, and how to make the most of their individual strengths and minimise their weaknesses.

'Would you believe they could improve so much in a few days?' Róisín marvelled.

'Magdawna looked surprised when he beat me by only one length yesterday,' Aidan said smugly. 'Not like the first practice race, when he won by three lengths.'

'I bet *I* could beat you in a chariot race,' Brona said. 'I don't see why you're the only one to practise against the queen's champion.'

'Why don't you try today, then? There's no reason why we shouldn't take turns.' Aidan knew that Brona was more than his match where horses were concerned.

'Will Magdawna mind if one of you beats him in a practice?' Rory asked. 'Surely no one should be able to beat the champion.'

'If we do beat him one day, it will only make him try

harder, and isn't that what all this practice is about?' Aidan replied. 'Why should he mind? Anyway, we'll see how Brona does today.'

In the late-afternoon sunshine, Magdawna drove his team out for the day's practice run. His red-gold hair hung in waves on his shoulders, against the whiteness of his charioteer's tunic. Maeve and Ailill stood on high ground where they could see the whole circuit. To keep her warm against the coolness of the day, the queen wore a cloak of woven wool dyed deep red, while Ailill had on a cloak of rich brown made from the skin of a young bear.

Brona, with the second team, drove up beside Magdawna and stopped her chariot with a flourish. She looked across at him. 'I won't be as easy on you as Aidan was,' she said with a grin.

Magdawna's violet eyes flashed as he laughed. 'The day I am beaten in practice is the day Maeve will need to appoint a new champion.'

Together they waited for the sound of the horn. When it came, they shot down the track together, all eight horses neck and neck until they reached the first bend. Brona's team lost ground here because she was on the outside. She knew that Magdawna would try to keep her on the outside, where she would fall further behind at each bend.

She decided to allow herself to lose a little more ground at each bend, until she was directly behind Magdawna's chariot; he could not see her there. To everyone watching, the situation looked much as it had when Aidan raced. Brona was falling behind and Magdawna was all set to win, racing powerfully in the centre of the track.

But Brona did not fall any further behind. She drove her team mercilessly at Magdawna's heels for lap after lap. Biding her time, she waited until the horn signalled that they were on the last lap, and heading down a long, straight stretch. *Now* Brona made her move. She urged her team to their greatest effort, bringing them to the inside of the track, where they gradually began to overtake Magdawna. At first he was not aware of how close Brona had come up behind him. When he realised what she was doing, it was too late. She was already forcing him further out, claiming the inside track for herself.

They raced neck and neck again, but not for long. Slowly Brona seized the advantage, and at the next bend she shot ahead of Magdawna. He tried to recover, but nothing could stop Brona now. Magdawna was on the outside and he had no chance to reclaim his inside position before the race was over. He had been outmanoeuvred. Brona was fully past the post with her horses and chariot before Magdawna began to cross the line. The impossible had happened: the queen's champion had been defeated.

No one cheered. Spectators waited to see how Maeve of the Thousand Spears would take her son's defeat. Brona slowed down her horses and Magdawna caught up with her. Together they wheeled around to face the queen. Both expected trouble: Magdawna for not winning, Brona because she had won.

Ailill spoke first. 'Well done, noble Brona,' he said. 'We are lucky to have you to teach us how to race. We manage our chariots well in battle, but we need different skills in competition.' He smiled and stroked his softly curling, golden beard.

Maeve's face was red with rage, but she took her cue from Ailill. 'We are fortunate to have such an expert horsewoman from a faraway place and a time yet unborn to help us,' she said coldly. 'I trust you can train my champion as well as you have trained our horses.'

Magdawna looked embarrassed. 'I thought strength and speed were everything,' he replied. 'I see now that I require more expertise and a degree of cunning.'

Brona bowed deeply from her chariot. 'We can make Magdawna unbeatable, Majesty. That is what you asked us to do, and that is what we are doing. Today was part of his lesson. He will never again be beaten by the same trick.'

'I have a suggestion,' Ailill said, bowing to Maeve. 'To make sure we have the best possible chance of winning this contest, I suggest that Aidan and Brona both compete in turn with our son, thus teaching him all they know. I suggest, too, that the second team is trained as well as Magdawna's own team. On the day of the race itself, when we have obtained permission from Datho, let us enter two champions. Our son will race as the queen's champion with his own team, and either Aidan or Brona will race as my champion. Whoever wins, the victory – and the trophy – will belong to Ardalba.'

Maeve thought about this. It seemed sensible, but why did Ailill suggest it? Was he still trying to prove he was better than she was, as he had tried to do when once, long ago, they had counted their possessions to see who was the richest? Even now, she meant one day to take the Brown Bull of Cooley from Lú, Lord of the North. When she had that, she would have a bull to match White Horn, Ailill's magnificent white bull, which would not allow itself to be owned by a woman and had joined Ailill's herd instead of hers. She would be delighted now if *her* champion, and not Ailill's, were to win Datho's contest. Of course Magdawna would triumph, she was sure of that. 'My husband,' she said at last, 'thank you for your wise counsel. It would be foolish of me to rely completely on one team of horses or on one Champion. We shall do as you suggest.'

Maeve turned on her heel and marched back into the fort without another word. Ailill winked at his son and Brona before turning to follow her. Magdawna and Brona gave their horses to their grooms, to take care of. Then the two friends went into the fort together. 'I really do have a lot to learn,' Magdawna admitted. 'Perhaps I could go with you to Boar Head Mountain and practise with you there?'

Brona remembered that Pooka had told them he wanted no one to know about his mountain, or about himself. To keep Pooka's secret, she could not agree to Magdawna's request. 'Most of our work on the mountain is to develop stamina and strength in the animals,' she said. 'We cannot use chariots on the slopes, so you would learn little if you joined us.'

Magdawna looked disappointed, but he said no more. Each evening he raced against Aidan or Brona, their teams well matched. It was a help to him to know that either Aidan or Brona would race with him on the day of competition.

On the last day of practice, the children met Pooka on the mountain as usual. 'Be careful,' he warned. 'Remember the threat of fire that Maeve saw through the Stone. Know this: if at any time you should need me, I will know, and I will come to you. You must say nothing, for only you will see me. I am invisible when I am off my mountain. You must not give away my presence.'

The children and all the horses said goodbye to Pooka and thanked him for his help. Then he blew fire into the nostrils of all Maeve's horses for the last time. Brona lingered behind the others to stroke Pooka's creamy-white mane. 'If I alone should ever call on you, Pooka, will Aidan, Róisín and Rory see you when you come to help me, or will you be visible to me only?' she asked.

'You are special, Brona,' Pooka replied softly. 'You, more

than the rest, are in tune with the Otherworld, where I live. If you ever need me, I will appear to you alone. And if you ever face a task full of danger, ask me for my gift of invisibility. I will bestow it on you alone. It will render you, what you wear and what you carry invisible to human eyes.'

Brona thanked the great Wild Horse of the Mountain and stroked his black forehead. Then she hurried after the others. The four children returned quickly to Ardalba to make themselves ready for the following day, and their long journey to Datho's fort.

# 6

## THE JOURNEY BEGINS

Maeve allowed three days to get to Datho's fort, leaving one day to rest and prepare the horses after they got there. She and all her court were ready to start at first light. The children had never seen anything like Maeve's cavalcade, of which today they were part. At the front strode two bodhrán players, who beat a steady, slow march. Behind them Maeve rode her own white battle charger, and Ailill rode on her right, accompanied by his standard-bearer, who held high Ardalba's white standard, showing its famous black-bull icon. Magdawna, as the prince and the queen's champion, sat his horse on her left, his attendant carrying his ceremonial shield and spear behind him.

Behind the royal party the children saw a crowd of high nobles stretching back to where they themselves walked. When Rory looked behind him, he saw that there were as many people behind him as there were in front. All the court attendants were there, followed by grooms, and by slaves tending packhorses loaded with provisions. Some grooms led Magdawna's racing team and the other teams of horses the children had trained. Slaves pulled the two racing chariots, covered in animal skins, on long trolleys.

'Wouldn't you say that this is much more than a chariot

race?' Aidan asked. 'It's more like a display of power. Look at the armed men all around us. No one would dare attack us.'

'Maeve wants everyone, in her own kingdom and outside it, to see her strength,' Róisín answered. 'She wants to be seen as the greatest monarch in Erin.'

'Isn't she that already?' Brona whispered. 'Why does she have to keep proving it?'

'What about Lú, Lord of the North?' Rory said. 'Isn't he roughly as powerful as Maeve?'

'That's what Maeve's afraid of,' Róisín said. 'That's why she knows she has to win this race. Winning really *is* a show of strength.'

Only the royal party and some of the guards were on horseback. The others walked along, talking, their speed kept uniform by the beat of the bodhrán. Soon Ardalba was far behind them. They were in open country, walking through grassland. Aidan suddenly pointed far to the front. 'There's Scathach. I thought Maeve would need her to stay close.'

The others saw Scathach striding along, a wolfhound on either side of her. Her dark-blue cloak swung behind her. She carried her druid's staff with the snake's-head design; the snake's emerald eyes glinted with a magical light. The children felt safer, knowing the powerful arch-druidess was with them.

The procession followed the route the children had taken on their previous journey. This time they travelled in comfort, sure they were taking the right path. During rest breaks, slaves offered them water and food. In the evening, attendants raised tents where they could take shelter for the night. Then everybody gathered round a huge fire for feasting and music. 'This time we can sleep without worrying about bears or wolves,' Rory said with satisfaction.

'And we don't have to think about spies, or whether we are being followed.' Brona sounded pleased. She could not forget the bear that once threatened to attack her.

*

Early in the next day's march they had to pass through a large wood full of oak, beech and elm. Trees grew closely, forcing Maeve's cavalcade to split up and continue in smaller groups.

'It was easier to keep together when there were only the four of us.' Aidan sounded grim. 'This crowd could easily get separated among the trees, and people could get lost.'

'Let's make sure *we* keep together no matter what,' Brona said. She remembered the time when they had lost Rory after he had been kidnapped, and when Brona had wandered off and later saved them from Ulcas Spellbinder.

'You're right,' Róisín said. 'This time we'll stay close and not lose sight of each other. Maybe the bodhráns are supposed to keep people from getting lost.'

When they were on their way after the midday break for food and rest, it seemed to the children that the forest had grown darker. Trees often cut out the light.

Then Rory began to sniff the air. 'Do you smell anything odd?' he asked the others.

They all sniffed. 'Maybe there's a charcoal burner somewhere near,' Aidan suggested.

That seemed a possibility. For the moment they thought no more about it. Then Brona saw movement ahead of them. 'Look,' she said. 'Why are those field mice running towards us?'

'Look up at the birds,' Róisín said, pointing to whole flocks flying overhead beneath the forest canopy. While she spoke, a hedgehog and a young badger came rushing past them.

'Something odd is happening,' Aidan said, looking uneasily around him. 'What do you think that noise is? It sounds as though it's far away.' A dull roar broke the stillness of the forest.

Rory spoke excitedly. 'I know what it is, it's the sound of a forest fire. That's the smoke we can smell.'

'How could we forget Scathach's warning about fire?' Brona said. 'This must be Archeld's doing.'

'We must warn Maeve,' said Aidan, 'and make sure the horses are safe.'

'And how do we do that when we don't know where the fire is?' asked Rory. The children looked around them through the trees but could see nothing, and they could not tell where the smell of smoke was coming from.

'If we found Scathach right away, it wouldn't help much,' Brona said. 'There hasn't been a full moon since Maeve consulted the Stone last, so she can't consult it again. There's no help there. What *can* we do?'

'Maeve can't consult her moonstone, but does that mean we can't consult ours?' Rory interrupted excitedly. 'Maeve and Scathach think that if the stone in Maeve's diadem can't be used, neither can any other moonstones in her kingdom. But shouldn't we at least try?'

'The only time we used the Stone on our own, we used two of our rings at the same time,' Brona said uncertainly.

'That's true,' Róisín agreed, 'but did we need to? Let's try with just one of us reading the Stone, using that person's ring on its own. If it works, we'll know we can use the other three rings as well before full moon.'

'It was my idea,' Rory reminded them. 'I should be the one to try.'

The others agreed to this and began to move quietly away from the rest of the party until they were hidden behind trees and could not be seen. Rory held up his ring, knelt down and got ready to read the Stone. Aidan stood in front of him to gaze into the ring Rory held out for him. 'Think of the Stone,' Aidan said. 'Clear your mind of other thoughts. See only the stone. Look into its liquid depths, where emerald, rose and gold glint and fade. See the colours. Watch them change.'

Rory concentrated until he saw the Stone in his mind's eye as clearly as if he was looking straight at it. Other thoughts faded. His breathing slowed. His whole consciousness was centred on the Stone.

'Now tell us what you see,' Aidan said.

Rory spoke in a muffled, trance-like voice, sounding as if he was far away. 'I see Maeve and Ailill. They are in front of everyone else. There is heavy smoke. They are gasping for breath.'

'Can you see the fire?' Aidan persisted. 'Can you see how far away it is from all of us?'

Rory did not reply for a moment. Then he said, 'Whole trees are blazing. I see their flaming trunks fall to the ground. Animals are trapped and cannot flee.'

'What else can you see?' Aidan tried to remain calm. 'Can you see a way past?'

Suddenly Rory spoke more loudly. 'It is in front of us, but far to the left. I see bodhrán players leading Maeve left to meet it. She cannot see through the smoke. We will die unless we turn away from it.'

Aidan took his eyes off Rory's ring when he heard that. Slowly Rory opened his eyes and looked around him. 'I know where the fire is,' he said. 'I can lead us all away from it.'

'We will tell no one how we learned about this,' Róisín warned. 'It is our secret.'

The children began to overtake those in front of them in

the procession as quickly as they could without causing alarm. Soon they caught up with Scathach and her wolfhounds. 'Noble Scathach,' Aidan said, 'there is fire ahead, perhaps started by Lú, as the Stone foretold. We are hurrying to warn Maeve and guide her past it.'

'I can smell it,' the arch-druidess replied. 'How can you guide the queen when we do not know where it rages?'

'We *do* know where it is,' Rory replied. 'We have our own way of learning such things.'

'Make haste then,' Scathach said, 'for surely no one else can now direct us to safety.'

The children hurried past Scathach and other senior nobles, until at last they reached Maeve, on her white horse behind the bodhrán players. 'Majesty,' Róisín called, 'we are heading into a fire. Let us guide you safely away from it.'

Maeve already had her cloak wrapped over her face to protect her from the smoke that blew more heavily over them with each passing minute. Ailill and Magdawna were coughing. The choking smoke caused everyone's eyes to water.

'Can you really help us?' the queen asked. 'My bodhrán players do not know which way to turn.'

'Follow us, Majesty. Let us lead you away from danger,' Rory said. He then moved out in front of the bodhrán players, with Aidan, Brona and Róisín walking three abreast behind him. Rory thought about exactly where he had seen the fire when he consulted the stone. They veered away to the right, leading the cavalcade in that direction.

Everyone could now hear the roaring of the flames. Wild creatures still tried desperately to escape the heat, which Maeve and the children began to feel blowing over them. The forest was growing darker because of the heavy black smoke. Now, far away to their left, they could all see the orange glow of flames.

Rory turned to Aidan and Brona. 'Go back and help the grooms,' he said. 'The horses will be difficult to lead through all this. Róisín will stay with me.'

The other three were not used to taking orders from Rory, but in Ardalba he spoke with conviction. Without a word, Aidan and Brona headed back past the nobles to where they found grooms struggling to control the four teams of horses which would carry Maeve's hopes of victory in Datho's race on the Plain of Mighty Stags.

# 7

## MAGDAWNA SLEEPS

Past high nobles and court attendants, all coughing as they followed Maeve through the smoke of the forest fire, Aidan and Brona walked back to where palace grooms led the horses. The grooms had wrapped damp cloths around the animals' heads to keep the smoke out of their lungs. The horses snorted through the smoke, tossing their heads and rolling their eyes in terror. The grooms spoke gently to them, holding their head-ropes firmly in an effort to stop them from rearing up or bolting.

'The poor things,' Brona said. 'This fire is dreadful for all of us, but at least we understand what's going on, and how to save ourselves.'

'Come on!' Aidan shouted over the roaring of the flames, which were getting closer. 'Let's give the grooms a hand. You stay with Magdawna's team. I'll go to the second team. That will free extra grooms for the spare teams.'

Until they were certain that the fire was behind them, Brona stayed with the champion's team, talking to them, calling each horse by name, stroking their long heads and calming them. Aidan did the same with the second team. They both knew that an upset like this could leave the animals unsettled and damage their chances in Datho's race.

'Perhaps Lú has done his worst now,' Brona called across to Aidan. 'If we have got through the fire that Maeve saw in the Stone, maybe he will do no more, thinking he has already spoiled Magdawna's chances of winning.'

'Don't be too sure,' Aidan answered. 'Lú does not give up easily, as we know all too well.' They both remembered Fiachart and how persistently he had pursued them, and how they would still be slaves to Ulcas Spellbinder, Archeld's apprentice druid, if Brona had not escaped to save them.

Gradually the smoke thinned out and they no longer heard the roaring of the flames. Little by little, the horses' panic lessened. The children rejoined the high nobles in Maeve's cavalcade. The danger from the fire was over.

*

When the forest was far behind them, Maeve decided they would stop to camp for the night beside a small stream. Magdawna and the children took the horses for a gallop to loosen them up after their long walk, and to help them forget the fire. Tomorrow they would reach Datho's fort, with one day left to relax and prepare for the contest.

'They ran well, everything considered,' Magdawna said, when he and the children returned to their tents. 'We'll use the chariots tomorrow, to make sure everything is in order, but we won't race the teams too hard. They need a day's rest to be at their best, and we don't want other competitors to witness how fast they can run.'

Everyone was worn out after the excitement of the day. The only people who did not sleep soundly until dawn were the guards whom the queen had appointed to stay alert in case of attack.

At sunrise the camp came to life again. Tents were folded

and the animals were fed and watered. The four children were getting excited about the race. So far they had thought only of training horses to run in it. At last they began to realise what a great event it would be and that they would have their place in it.

'It's the biggest competition that has ever been held in the whole land,' Róisín said, with wonder in her voice. 'And we will be part of it.'

'That's why Maeve wants so badly to win,' Rory replied. 'It's an international race. You heard all the places from which people are coming to compete. The winner will be famous far and wide.'

'I don't know about people from other lands,' Aidan said, sounding worried, 'but we have Lord Lú of the North to think about. He'll do anything he can to make sure he wins.'

'Lú doesn't know that one of *us* will be racing,' Brona reminded him, 'or that Maeve hopes to enter two teams. He'll concentrate on spoiling things for the prince, won't he?'

After a rest for food, the cavalcade continued its march until Datho's fort came into sight. Shining in the afternoon sunlight, it looked even more magnificent than the four children had remembered it. As large as Ardalba itself, the enclosure stood high on a hillside ahead of them, protecting many circular dwellings within its stockade. Pieces of mica in the granite walls of Datho's palace glittered like diamonds, giving the building a magical radiance.

Aidan couldn't take his eyes off it. 'I'll never forget the first time we saw that palace,' he said.

'Look!' Brona pointed excitedly down into the valley they had to cross to reach the fort. The ground was covered with brightly coloured tents. There were people everywhere, and near each tent stood a team of horses. There seemed to be at least five or six teams present, and there was a whole day left for the others to arrive. None of the children had ever seen anything like it.

Maeve's cavalcade moved down into the valley until it reached the King's Highway, a wide road such as no one had seen elsewhere, but which the children had walked on when they first came to Dara Mór. When they approached the entrance to the fort, Datho himself came out to meet them, his herald at his side. The children had not forgotten how, on their last visit in the guise of slaves, they had to wait outside the gate with Samhain the silversmith.

The herald, dressed in a pale-blue tunic and a cloak of the amber yellow used by members of Datho's household, proclaimed: 'Welcome to Maeve of the Thousand Spears, wife of Ailill, King of the West, Keeper of the Moonstone, Guardian of the Black Bull of Wisdom, Great Ruler of Ardalba that stretches as far as Shining River.'

Then Datho stepped forward. 'Majesty,' he said, 'I welcome you to my home, and invite you and your family to stay here with me in my palace. Your people may set their tents near at hand on the even ground at the foot of this hillside.'

'That is gracious of you, Datho,' Maeve replied, 'but before I accept your offer to lodge at your fort, may I ask what arrangements you have made for Lú? I do not wish to sleep beneath the same roof as my enemy.'

Datho smiled. 'Lú has not yet arrived. When he does, I will appoint for his use land that is not within sight of the fort. You need not fear meeting him before the race.'

'Then I thank you,' Maeve said with a relieved laugh, 'and we gladly accept your hospitality.'

'I will hold a feast for all,' Datho said. 'Outside on the lower slopes. Should Lú attend the feast, I cannot prevent an accidental encounter.'

The children helped Magdawna and the grooms to settle the horses for the night, making sure that guards would watch over them at all times. Magdawna then joined his parents at Datho's fort. The four children found where their loyal attendants had set up tents for them. The attendants helped the children wash off the dust of the journey before dressing their hair in court style once more and helping them put on their high nobles' rich garments and jewels in preparation for the feast.

Much later, after everybody had eaten plenty of the good food provided by Datho, the singing and storytelling began. Musicians from far lands played strange music on unusual instruments. Great Celtic harpers answered them with songs of amazing deeds, especially those of Maeve and Datho. Storytellers spun their tales, some tragic, some bringing great gales of laughter from their listeners. At last the listeners began to slip away to their tents for the night. Aidan, Róisín, Brona and Rory were among the first to go.

*

Next morning they were out early with Magdawna to test that the chariots were in order and that the horses were fit. Rory checked all the moving parts of the chariots. 'Everything is as good as new,' he told the prince. 'Both chariots are in perfect condition.'

Magdawna ordered slaves to polish his queen's champion's chariot until its gleaming oak wood shone and its ivory inlays gleamed white. Aidan and Brona attended to Maeve's own chariot, which one of them would use if Datho allowed her two entries to the race. They burnished the embossed silver that covered its sides until it shone in the sunlight.

'Let's get the teams harnessed,' Magdawna suggested, 'just

to make sure that everything works and that we have forgotten nothing.'

'Wouldn't it be better to wait until the cool of the evening for that?' Brona asked. 'Then we could give the horses a short practice as well.'

'You're right,' Magdawna answered. 'We know the chariots are all right and will look magnificent for the race, so let's give ourselves and the horses the day off.'

Ardalba's prince returned to the fort. The children decided to look around the whole encampment. They had not gone far when Rory saw Samhain. With him was his son Cormac. 'Samhain!' Rory yelled. 'Cormac!'

Datho's master silversmith saw them at once and smiled broadly. 'My favourite high nobles,' he said. 'What are you doing here?'

'Maeve hopes to win Datho's Bowl,' they said. 'We helped to train the horses for the race.'

'There would be no Datho's Bowl if noble Rory had not risked his life to recover it from Cruachan's thieving hands,' Samhain said. 'I've travelled here to see it one more time, in case someone from across the sea should win it and take it home with him.'

'We at the crannóg remember you, and fisherfolk tell tales of your deeds,' Cormac told them. 'None of us will ever forget how you saved my father's life.' They promised to meet again after the feast that would follow the race.

The children continued their inspection of the camping area. They looked closely at the horses and chariots from distant kingdoms, noting the ones they thought would do well. In many cases they saw the champions too, all tall men with strong muscles and great confidence. 'How could I ever race against *them*?' Brona whispered to the others. 'They are bigger and stronger than me.'

'Size and strength aren't what counts,' Rory reminded her. 'Magdawna is stronger than you, and you beat him, didn't you?'

'I feel nervous too,' Aidan confessed. 'They look really tough. And look at their huge brutes of horses!'

'How do they treat their horses?' Róisín asked. 'Ours respond to kindness and encouragement. Perhaps they trained theirs with the whip. Horses who fear their masters do not put their hearts into running well, do they?'

'Not one of *their* horses was trained by Pooka, the Wild Horse of the Mountain,' Rory pointed out. 'We have the advantage.'

'And there isn't much time left for Lú to damage them by fire,' said Róisín. 'He hasn't arrived yet.'

That was true. By now, contestants had reached the plain from far and wide, but there was still no sign of Lú, Lord of the North. Nor did he appear during the remainder of the day. 'Some accident must have delayed him,' Aidan surmised. 'He is as determined to win this race as Maeve is.'

When the air grew cool in the late afternoon, Magdawna appeared again, with Maeve and Ailill. They called the four children together. 'We have permission from Datho to enter two teams tomorrow,' Maeve announced. 'I want you all to know that I have chosen Brona for the second team. She has defeated Magdawna fairly many times in practice runs. She can coax the best out of the horses.'

Aidan, Rory and Róisín turned to congratulate Brona. Aidan hid his disappointment that he would not race; he knew in his heart that Brona was better for the job than he was.

'Win or lose,' Maeve continued, 'I thank all of you for your hard work in preparing the animals to run tomorrow. Now we would like to watch your last practice with the chariots.'

Magdawna and Brona had arranged for grooms to have the chariots ready at the freshly sanded course Datho had prepared. Maeve, Ailill and her attendants went with them to watch. 'Will we go round the course once or twice?' Brona asked Magdawna.

'What do you think, Brona?' Magdawna replied. He had great respect for Brona's horsemanship.

'I think once is enough,' she answered. 'We don't want to let other teams see too much. Let's do it at a stately pace that will give the impression that our horses are heavy and not too fast.'

'Good idea,' Magdawna said.

When a groom dipped a standard to start them off, Brona and Magdawna were ready. The chariots shot off at a fair gallop, staying side by side for the whole distance. Maeve and her party were waiting for them when the lap was done. Magdawna and Brona reined in the teams and came to a stop.

'The horses looked as though they were wading through honey,' Aidan called.

'That's what we wanted them to look like,' Brona said. 'We want people to think they're slower than they really are.'

Grooms approached to take the horses and chariots away. Brona stepped down and handed hers over. Magdawna began to step down from his chariot, but as his foot touched the ground, without warning he stumbled and fell. Then he lay on the ground without moving.

'Magdawna!' Maeve cried, running to him. He did not stir or look at her, though strangely, his eyes were wide open. Maeve wrung her hands in despair. 'Carry him to a tent,' she ordered. 'My champion cannot be seen like this on the eve of the great race.'

'Take him to *my* tent,' Aidan offered. 'It's the nearest.'

Attendants came to carry their prince to the shelter of Aidan's tent, out of sight of strangers. Maeve and Ailill walked on either side of him, alarmed at the sudden, dreadful collapse of their son. The four children, deeply shocked, followed them in silence.

# 8

## THE CONTEST BEGINS

In Aidan's tent, attendants carefully laid the prince on a bed of soft animal skins. Róisín rolled up Aidan's spare cloak to make a pillow for their friend's head. Maeve knelt beside him and gently stroked his forehead, which was hot as if with fever. Magdawna's eyes stared blankly straight upwards. He did not respond to his mother or to the presence of those around him.

Maeve spoke in low tones of grief. 'My son, what has befallen you?' Ailill stood beside her, his hand on her shoulder to comfort her.

Attendants brought warm water to bathe Magdawna's face and burnt sharp-smelling herbs to try to restore him to consciousness. Nothing worked. He lay unmoving, his cheeks flushed.

'Majesty,' Róisín said softly, not wanting to intrude. Maeve looked around at her blankly, too upset to speak. 'Majesty, could this unusual sleep of Magdawna have anything to do with Lord Lú? Could his feverish state be the fire we have feared from the start?'

Maeve's violet eyes focused sharply on Róisín while she took in the meaning of her words. 'This is not the fire I saw in the Stone,' she replied. 'That was bright and blinding.

But why would Lú stop at the forest fire, which we are lucky to have survived? This could well be another evil attack of his, or of his anti-druid Archeld.'

She stood up from the still form of her son. Now she was thinking like a queen again, as well as like a mother. 'You are right, Noble Róisín,' she said. 'We must never forget the dark power of Lú.' She turned to her attendant. 'Pray summon noble Scathach, arch-druidess of Ardalba, to my presence,' she commanded. 'I shall wait for her here with Ailill.'

When Scathach arrived this time there were no bodhráns to announce her. She had brought no wolfhounds. It was obvious that she had heard of Magdawna's collapse from the attendant and had hurried immediately to Maeve's side, waiting only to fetch her druidic staff. 'Majesty,' she gasped, out of breath, 'what has happened?'

After Maeve had told Scathach how Magdawna had fallen, and the arch-druidess had observed his staring eyes and lack of consciousness, Scathach spoke with authority: 'Archeld has cast a spell on him. I would recognise his work anywhere. Archeld's nasty apprentice, Ulcas Spellbinder, could also have done it. But the person behind it all is definitely Lord Lú of the North.'

'Is it within your power to break this spell, noble Scathach?' Maeve asked nervously. She knew all too well what strong spells Archeld cast. An anti-druid helped people only when, by helping them, he could harm others: he would help Lú because Lú would then harm Maeve.

'It may be that this spell is beyond my power to undo,' Scathach replied. 'I will not know that until I try.' She turned to her attendant, who had followed her to Aidan's tent. 'Please fetch my hazel rod, and be quick.'

In no time, the girl returned with the hazel rod. Scathach had everyone stand away from Magdawna. With the rod, she scratched a line in the earthen floor of the tent, making a circle around him. When she had completed the circle, she paused with closed eyes to summon up her power. Then she stepped inside the circle and in loud tones commanded Magdawna, 'Scathach bids you wake.' He did not stir. Scathach tried again, and then a third time. Still Magdawna lay unmoving.

Then Scathach turned to Brona. 'When I broke Ulcas's spell on the island,' she said, 'you and I focused our power together. Will you come into the circle with me now to help Magdawna?'

Brona felt herself blushing. She did not know that she had any special power – none like Scathach's, anyway. 'Of course I will,' she said, 'but all the power was yours the last time.'

Scathach held Brona's hand while they both closed their eyes to gather their strength. Together they stepped into the hazel-rod circle and said loudly, 'Scathach bids you wake.' Magdawna did not move at first. Then, a moment later, he closed his eyes and turned away from them.

'I cannot help you, Majesty,' Scathach said to Maeve with regret in her voice. 'Magdawna is now in a deep sleep, far deeper than normal. He will not wake until the spell is spent. We both know that that will not happen until after the start of tomorrow's race. You are without a racing champion.' She bowed deeply to the queen and left the tent.

Maeve looked around her. 'Some day I will fight battles with Lú,' she said darkly, 'and the Brown Bull of Cooley will not be the only reason for war.'

'The race is tomorrow,' Ailill reminded her. 'You need to decide what you will do without Magdawna for your champion.'

'You are right, husband,' Maeve replied. She stood over her son, lost in thought for several moments. Then, her decision made, she turned to Ailill and the four children.

'Noble Brona,' she said, 'you were to race the second team against my son and the other contestants. Will you consent to be my champion tomorrow and race Magdawna's team for the honour of Ardalba?'

Brona stared at Maeve, unable at first to reply. Racing the second team was one thing; the responsibility of being the queen's champion was something else. Could she do it? What if she failed? But she knew in her heart that she was better with horses than anyone else Maeve could call on.

Bowing deeply to Ardalba's ruler, Brona answered in low tones: 'You honour me by your trust, Majesty. I am privileged that you choose me to be your champion. I will race Magdawna's team as well as I can, and hope I will win the trophy for Ardalba.'

Maeve smiled for the first time since Magdawna had fallen. 'Thank you,' she said. 'We are fortunate to have all of you, with your strength and authority from a faraway place and a time yet unborn, to help us in times of difficulty.' The others were pleased for Brona, feeling glad that one of them, from a small place like Glenelk, was going to race as Ardalba's champion against people from lands far and wide.

Maeve then turned to Aidan. 'Noble Aidan, we may still race two teams,' she said. 'Will you race the second team for me, as Ailill's champion?'

Bowing deeply, Aidan could not hide his delight at Maeve's request. 'Thank you for choosing me, Majesty,' he said. 'I will race as well as I can, although I am not likely to defeat your new champion.'

'No,' Maeve answered with a smile, 'you are not likely to do that, but we run the second team in case something prevents the champion from racing, as has happened to my son, or in case of an accident to the horses or the chariot. We are lucky to have people so experienced with horses to take his place.' Maeve and Ailill left. Magdawna remained to be cared for in Aidan's tent, because Maeve did not want her son seen by strangers in his present state.

The four children began to make plans. They decided they would get up early the next day to take the horses for a canter to loosen them up. Then Rory would again go over every inch of the two chariots to check for mechanical problems and Róisín would give them a final polish.

*

Next morning there was great activity throughout the camp. Some new contestants had arrived the previous evening, and more were still to come. 'Where's Lú?' Róisín asked. 'He'll never miss the race and the chance it gives him to humiliate Ardalba.'

'After all his fires and spells, he thinks it will be a walkover,' Rory said, laughing. 'He's in for a shock, isn't he?'

In the early part of the morning they attended to the horses' needs. By noon the children had checked the chariots and left guards with them until the race. Brona and Aidan then went to their tents to get ready. Their attendants dressed their hair. Brona's black, straight hair, fringed and cut short, was oiled and gleaming. Róisín thought she looked unbeatable – strong, businesslike and capable. Aidan's sandy locks, trimmed at the back of his neck, marked him out from the other contestants, who all seemed to have long hair falling below their shoulders.

Brona wore her own charioteer's white tunic, with worked leather greaves to guard her shins. The gold medallion which marked her out as the queen's champion was on a chain round her neck. Aidan, too, wore a white tunic. For the opening parade they both wore long white cloaks: white was Ardalba's distinguishing colour. Outside their tents they could hear a clamour from the assembled crowds. Each party was in the last stages of their preparations, giving orders to grooms, harnessing horses and shouting across to friends.

While Brona and Aidan got dressed for the race, Rory and Róisín were putting the finishing touches to the horses. They brushed them until their white coats gleamed, brushed out their tails, and combed and tied up their manes so that they did not fall over the horses' eyes. Then they harnessed the teams to their chariots and led them to the waiting area. Charioteers came out to stand with their teams. Incredibly, there was still no sign of Lú.

Soon it was time to line up for the solemn parade around the course. Standing erect in their chariots, their cloaks billowing behind them in the breeze, Aidan and Brona felt as if they would burst with pride and excitement. The race-master blew his horn to get the contestants in line. When everyone was ready, he blew again to get the parade under way. It was a wonderful sight. Róisín and Rory felt proud of Aidan and Brona. Their banner, showing Ardalba's Black Bull of Wisdom on a white background, fluttered above their heads. Side by side, their well-groomed white teams looked outstanding, gaining a shout of approval from onlookers. When they passed Maeve and the Ardalba party, everyone stood up to clap them on.

Seven other contestants carried their standards proudly before the company. Sualtham from Sarum, his fair hair tied back, his face painted in ceremonial patterns in startling blue woad, caught everyone's eye. He bore the proud standard of Sarum embroidered with standing stones set in a circle and supporting heavy boulders. His partner in the parade was Falga from Man, whose cloak and standard were both in the distinctive violet of his homeland.

Next came Eric from the Northern Lands. His horned helmet sat over his shaggy blond hair, which fell down his back. His standard displayed an iris-yellow circle on a navy background to represent the midnight sun seen in his country. His cloak was a brilliant yellow, and his face bore three yellow slashes on each cheek. His partner was Diarmuid from Aran in a cloak of grey homespun; his banner, which was also grey, depicted a mighty salmon.

After them came Scotus from Caledonia, whose cloak and standard were of black-and-green tartan. Beside him, Penardun of the Land of Dragons proudly held the red dragon on his standard and wore a magnificent red cloak. Behind them was Oginran from Tintagel, his brown banner embroidered in silver thread with two crossed swords. His partner was missing: Lú had still not appeared.

'This is a huge course,' Brona called over to Aidan. 'It must be nearly a mile around.'

'You're right,' Aidan agreed, 'and we have to go round it ten times.'

The chariots and teams continued at a walk around the course, so that everyone watching could admire the display. Datho wanted people to remember the spectacle for as long as they lived.

Stewards now put each team into its proper position for the start, in places that had been decided by lot. They were a magnificent sight, nine teams standing side by side waiting for the signal. Brona and Aidan were beside each other near the centre of the line, with four teams outside Brona's. When all was ready, the starter took his place.

Then murmurs began at the edge of the watching crowd and slowly grew to become a roar. Brona and Aidan heard what the crowd was shouting: 'Lord Lú! Lord Lú! Hold the race for Lú! Lú is coming!'

# 9

## THE FIERY CHARIOT

'I told you he'd turn up,' Brona called to Aidan. 'I knew he wouldn't miss this race.'

Stewards delayed the start, waiting for Lú to approach. He swept up on a powerful chestnut horse, escorting his chariot – with its team of large, black stallions – driven by Fiachart, his champion. Riding with Lú was Archeld, his anti-druid, holding his druidic staff like a spear. None of the children had ever seen Lú before. In his black cloak and riding tunic, he looked big and menacing.

'See who Lú's champion is?' Rory muttered to Róisín, from their place in the watching crowd. 'I'd hoped we would never meet *him* again.'

'If he cheats as well as he lies, Brona and Aidan had better watch out,' she replied. None of them would ever forget how Fiachart's lies had got them all imprisoned by Datho's Steward of the West when they brought the Black Bull of Wisdom to him for safekeeping.

Fiachart drew up to the starting line in his gleaming chariot adorned with silver panels. He viciously reined his horses to a stop. He was right on the outside, the fifth chariot away from Brona. His deep-red standard fluttering behind him was embroidered with Lú's Black Hand emblem. When she saw that Fiachart was Lú's champion, Brona knew that he would stop at nothing to win.

Lú went with Archeld to a spot far away from the other spectators, where he sat on his horse to watch the race. Then the starter took his place once more. When he dropped the starter's banner, his assistant blew loudly on his horn and the teams were off.

Brona and Aidan had never done anything as exciting as this. They had removed their long white cloaks at the end of the parade. They stood braced now against the front of their chariots, feeling the speed of the chariots and the wind blowing their tunics tight against them. They felt free and powerful; they thought they could do anything. Their arms were stretched out straight ahead of them clutching the reins; they raced their teams neck and neck and for a moment forgot the rest of the field. But not for long! Suddenly spectators gave a loud shout of alarm. Brona and Aidan wondered what was in store for them.

Rory and Róisín, on the sidelines, saw it all. As soon as the race had started, they observed Lú's chariot turn into a ball of fire, or so it seemed. It was as bright as the sun, so that when anyone looked at it, they felt blinded by its brightness. Maeve, watching with the children, gave a loud gasp. 'That's the fire the stone showed me,' she said. 'I recognise it too late. What does it mean?'

'It means Archeld's evil work, Majesty.' Scathach, who stood beside the queen, looked grim. 'We are helpless against it, and must wait to see its purpose.'

Meanwhile, Fiachart drove his team madly until he drew level with Penardun from the Land of Dragons in the chariot next to him, as if he intended to overtake him. Penardun, suddenly blinded by Fiachart's fiery chariot, lost control of his frightened horses. They strained in different directions until the chariot overturned, throwing the charioteer to the ground and leaving his proud banner in the dust.

As the second lap began, Fiachart, the only person who seemed not to be blinded by the brilliant light of his own chariot, brought his chariot closer and closer to the next team on his left, driven by Falga from Man. That driver too gave a shout of despair as he realised that he could not manage his terrified animals. They bolted, and Falga's chariot met the same fate as Penardun's, overturning and throwing its driver to the ground.

Stewards carried off Falga and Penardun, who were wounded and unconscious, and sent some of Datho's slaves to catch the runaway horses. Brona knew that only two chariots remained between her and Fiachart. She tried to remain in the lead, but her horses sensed that all was not well. Their eyes rolled back to see what was behind them, and they fell out of step with each other. Brona was terrified at the thought of being thrown from a bucking chariot. Light from the fiery chariot was blinding her, as Fiachart began to come abreast of the next chariot on her right. Although her horses were distracted, Brona urged her team on, and they pulled slightly ahead.

At that moment, Fiachart caught up with the chariot on his left. Its driver was Eric from the Northern Lands, still wearing his horned helmet. He and his horses were blinded by the fiery chariot, as Penardun and Falga had been. His chariot also overturned, and he was thrown to the dust. Now only one chariot, that of Oginran from Tintagel, remained between Brona and Fiachart.

All the horses were running flat out by this time. Brona lost sight of Aidan. Her attention was to her right, where the menace of Lú remained. Would Oginran be the next to fall, and how much longer could she hold out? In the middle of her distress, she remembered Pooka and his promise. She had no strength to call aloud to him, only to send him her thoughts: *Pooka, I need you now. Pooka, help me.*

In a moment there he was, galloping ahead of her, his white mane and tail flying, his black coat gleaming. He was visible to Brona and the horses but to no one else. Pooka ran in front of the team, and Brona could hear his voice coming back to her through the noise of the race and the crowds: *Brona, keep your eyes on me and you will succeed. No fire will harm you.*

She forgot Fiachart. Pooka, Wild Horse of the Mountain, swifter than any mortal horse, ran ahead of her. Brona's team remembered how he had trained them, and they followed him. No one could catch them now. For lap after lap they stayed in the lead. Fiachart could not harm them from behind. He got no further chance to come abreast of them, where he could blind them.

Soon the contestants saw that only one green banner remained, telling them they were on the final lap. Brona was now one chariot-length ahead of Aidan, and three chariot-lengths ahead of Fiachart. Aidan's horses too had seen Pooka and had followed him. With the winning post in sight, Brona, whose eyes were still firmly fixed on Pooka, saw him leave the ground and gallop higher and higher up into the clouds, until she could see him no more.

Then she was past the finishing post, winner of the trophy for Ardalba, and champion charioteer of the west.

# 10

## DATHO'S FEAST

Brona allowed her horses to slow down until they came to a stop. She could hear the roar of the spectators, which she had been unaware of during the contest. Brona could scarcely believe that she had got safely to the end of the race in spite of Lú and his evil anti-druid, and that the trophy was really hers and would go to Ardalba.

Aidan's chariot pulled up beside hers and she could hear him shouting, 'Well done! Well done!' He looked as pleased as if he had won the trophy himself. Their grooms appeared beside them to hold the horses' heads.

Brona turned to look for the fiery chariot, which had wrought so much havoc among the contestants, and had left her terrified. But there *was* no fiery chariot, only Fiachart pulling a sad black wreck to the side of the course. Lú's four black stallions stood shivering and sweating.

Grooms led the children's white horses around in a circle so that Brona and Aidan could drive back to the platform from which Datho had watched the race. Many of his high nobles stood with him, waiting for him to confer honours on those who had won them.

Brona walked her horses until they were directly in front of Datho. Aidan wheeled his to stand on her right. Third place went to Sualtham from Sarum, who stood his chariot on Brona's left. Sualtham's face, still decorated with ceremonial blue markings, did not look menacing, as it had before the race, but was smiling and proud at the same time. He held his blue standard high in his left hand, the impressive stone circle embroidered on its folds fluttering valiantly in the breeze.

'How did you get past the fiery chariot?' Brona asked him.

'I do not know,' he replied. 'I started on the inside track. When your teams pulled forward so strongly, the black team drawing the fiery chariot slowed down. At the same time, the brightness of its fire began to dim.'

Brona said no more to Sualtham. She thought about what had happened and decided that Pooka had been as responsible for Fiachart's horses slowing down as he had been for her team and Aidan's running more strongly.

Datho stood high on his platform in front of his people and gestured for silence. When all were quiet, he spoke. 'I declare noble Brona, queen's champion for Ardalba, to be the winner of today's contest. I call now on Maeve of the Thousand Spears to step forward to receive my trophy, which people call Datho's Bowl. Then I will bestow the victor's prize on Brona.'

Maeve walked up to Datho and bowed low before him. Ailill stood by her side with Magdawna, who was now fully recovered from his sudden collapse. As Scathach had foretold, he had woken from his enchanted sleep the moment the race started, and had come to watch it. 'I am honoured to receive this glorious trophy for Ardalba,' Maeve said, accepting the bowl. 'I will treasure it at my court. There we shall always know it as Datho's Bowl. Your name enhances it, noble lord, and will remind me daily of your friendship, which is precious to me and to my people.'

Datho handed the great silver bowl to Maeve, then walked across to Brona where she stood in her chariot, her queen's-champion medallion glinting in the sunlight. Around her neck he hung an amber ribbon that had a sparkling oval pendant hanging on it. 'I congratulate you on a bravely run race,' Datho said, 'a race run in the face of difficulty and danger which none of us had foreseen. It gives me great pleasure to make this award, and I declare your right henceforth to wear my colour whenever it may help you to do so, and to call on me should danger threaten and my power could protect you.'

Brona was delighted by Datho's generosity. 'Thank you, noble Datho,' she said. 'I will always treasure your friendship.'

Maeve then spoke to the assembled gathering. 'I wish to thank noble Brona for carrying my colour so successfully to victory in this race. Lú's anti-druid, Archeld, put my son, who was my champion, under a sleep-spell at the last moment. I called on Brona to take his place, and all in Ardalba are now in debt to her. She will be known henceforth as the queen's champion.'

Everyone cheered and clapped Brona's achievement, and they went on cheering and clapping until she thought they would never stop. She felt embarrassed by all this attention. She was relieved when Datho left her to present winners' awards to Aidan, for second place, and to Sualtham, for third.

After the presentations, Datho spoke once more to the assembly. 'What ruler in all the land could produce two teams of strong horses like Maeve's?' he asked. 'And what ruler prepared two spare champions, as she wisely did?'

There was loud applause and shouting from the crowd at this. Róisín and Rory shouted louder than the rest, so proud were they of Aidan and Brona.

Datho gestured once more for silence. 'To celebrate the

victory of Ardalba's champion, to welcome contestants from faraway lands and to honour my friend Maeve of the Thousand Spears, I now invite all of you to a feast at my fort. We will enjoy food, company, music, poetry and storytelling until a new day dawns.' The whole gathering cheered and shouted their delight at Datho's invitation. Then they drifted off to prepare for the festivities to come.

Meanwhile, Lú, standing far away beyond the crowd, was not cheering. He knew that, by what he had done in the race, he had lost face among the people of his own land and of lands far across the sea. He determined to do what he could from now on to damage Maeve. He marched back in a fury to where he had secretly raised his tent. When he got there, he called for his anti-druid, Archeld. 'What do you say now about your fiery chariot?' he demanded. 'It was supposed to make sure that *I* would win, not Maeve's champion. And what was your idea in putting a spell on Magdawna, when you let that girl win instead of him?'

'Noble Lú,' Archeld replied, 'during the race, magic stronger than mine was at work. I know not from where it came. I am certain it slowed our horses and made them falter. And Magdawna was the only one I *could* put a spell of sleep on. I did not know whom Maeve might choose in his stead.' He bowed low before his master.

'The harm is done,' Lú conceded grudgingly. 'What do you suggest now?'

'Noble master, there is no need for Datho's Bowl to travel west with Maeve, when it could travel north with us.'

Lú smiled derisively. 'How do we get it, to take it north?' he asked.

'That is exactly what we do,' Archeld said. 'We *take* it.'

'You mean *steal* it? With all these people about?'

'The feasting will continue until dawn,' Archeld said.

'During that time, I have power to cast the whole company into a heavy sleep, as I did with Magdawna, and keep them asleep until tomorrow's sunrise. What better time to take the trophy? It will soon be in Maeve's room at the fort, wrapped in its travelling furs. We will have from the moment my spell comes into effect until tomorrow morning to take it and bear it north with us.'

Lú considered this. '*You* steal it, then,' he said. 'If you're caught, I'll say I know nothing about it. I'll strike camp later and leave here as soon as the feast gets under way. When the revelry is at its loudest, cast your spell. Seize the trophy from the fort and follow me. I'll leave a fast chariot for you, with a charioteer.' Archeld left Lú and went to where he could watch the fort and the festivities taking place outside it. He set himself to wait until the noise from the feasting had built to a crescendo.

Róisín decided to check on Penardun, Falga and Eric, whose chariots had been overturned by Lú's fiery chariot. Eric's horned helmet had protected his head from injury, but he was still bruised all over. Falga and Penardun had both been knocked out and were feeling weak. Róisín advised those tending to the wounded charioteers to make them rest for a while. When she was sure that the wounded were relaxing and getting over their knocks, she left them to go and help Aidan and Brona.

'And how's the queen's champion today?' she asked with a laugh, going into Brona's tent.

Brona laughed too. 'I'm all right,' she said, 'but now I'm beginning to stiffen up. Ten miles in a chariot with no springs can leave you shaken.'

Róisín decided that Brona and Aidan needed a quick swim in the river that ran by the camping ground. When they came out of the water, Róisín went back with Brona to her tent, telling Rory to go with Aidan. Then she rubbed some aromatic oil that Scathach had given her into Brona's legs and arms, which were tired after the race. In Aidan's tent, Rory did the same for him. Both Brona and Aidan felt their muscles relax under the influence of the healing herbal extracts in the oil.

While they were all resting, they could hear the preparations for the night's revelries getting under way. 'Hadn't we better be getting ready for the feast?' Aidan asked, as soon as he began to feel more energetic.

Back in Róisín's tent, Áilne combed out her mistress's long chestnut hair, dividing it into sections which she worked into several thin plaits, ornamented with gold beads. Róisín's full-length russet gown of fine linen was heavily embroidered with gold thread, and held in place with gold bodice clasps and a belt woven of gold threads. Her iris-yellow cloak flowed around her, held by a heavy gold shoulder brooch.

Áilne then assisted Brona, and because she was the champion, the attendant dressed her more elaborately still. She brushed Brona's jet-black hair, which was always too short for Ardalba fashions, until it shone. She combed her heavy fringe from her face and held it with a circlet of gold encrusted with amethysts, which sat on her forehead like a crown. Brona's dress was the colour of amethyst, her cloak a contrasting leaf-green.

Aidan and Rory were as splendid-looking as Brona and Róisín. To mark the fact that he had come second in the race, Aidan wore a gold-braided mantle over a tunic interwoven with threads of gold. Round his neck rested a golden torque, beautifully twisted, its workmanship worthy of Samhain himself, and on his shoulder he displayed a brooch of gold with a glowing amber stone at its heart.

Rory looked almost as brilliant. His white tunic had gold embroidery round the neck, and heavy gold fringes. Over it he wore a sleeveless jacket of rich red, with gold clasps instead of buttons. His cloak was midnight blue, a shade that complemented the red of his red jacket. It was held at his shoulder by a richly jewelled brooch.

Neither Aidan nor Rory could do anything with their hair, because it was too short. Ardalban men all wore their hair long. Aidan's came down to just below his ears. He made his attendants prepare it like that because he thought his ears stuck out. Rory's hair came to the tops of his ears, and he had it cut in a straight line from there across the tops of his eyebrows. It looked like a cap of red gold. They both looked so different from other men at court that their short hair gave them added distinction.

When they were ready, the children met outside their tents. They could hardly recognise each other in such rich clothing. 'You two look terrific,' Aidan told Brona and Róisín. 'I've never seen you look so beautiful.'

Róisín and Brona laughed at Aidan's compliment and twirled in circles so that their cloaks floated around them. 'You both look great too,' Brona said. 'Every bit as good as other high nobles, whether they are Maeve's or Datho's.'

'Isn't Aidan's gold collar terrific?' Rory asked the girls. 'I wish I had one.'

'Datho and Maeve are generous to lend us such precious jewels and clothes,' Brona said. 'We couldn't wear our jeans and anoraks for this kind of state occasion.'

For the feast, slaves had arranged a bank of dried grass in a great circle for people to sit on. In front of this they had put a series of low wooden tables, on which they had placed small loaves of bread in shallow straw baskets, and wooden bowls full of tiny cakes made with honey and nuts. They laid out drinking vessels at intervals, together with flagons of mead and great jugs of spring water.

The feast could not begin until Datho, having taken his place in the circle, announced the start of the festivities. On either side of him, people took their seats in order of rank. When the children approached, attendants were waiting to lead them to their places. Maeve was sitting on Datho's left hand, with Ailill and Magdawna beside her. Brona, as champion, sat on Datho's right. There was much shouting and cheering when those present recognised in this magically dressed girl the tough champion who had that afternoon driven her team of white horses to victory. Aidan sat on her right. Rory and Róisín were together, further along the table.

First, Datho's slaves poured mead from large jugs. Other slaves brought in food on huge wooden platters. Savoury smells rose from enormous cauldrons, some containing stewed meat, others soup seasoned with herbs. Then joints of pork and venison were brought to the guests. Finally, two attendants carried in a spit-roasted boar on a gleaming bronze shield and placed it in front of Brona. She was today's champion and had the honour to make – and eat – the first cut. She looked at the boar in fascination.

'Go on,' Datho said. 'They are all waiting until you serve yourself.'

Brona looked at the enormous joint, whirls of aromatic steam rising from it. How was she supposed to carve a piece out of that? Datho saw her dilemma. Brona had no sword, such as other champions would carry to a feast. He turned to his sword-bearer, who was standing behind him, and pulled out a dagger with a sharp iron blade. The dagger usually hung in its own small scabbard from the bronze scabbard holding his sword. 'Cut it with this,' he said. 'Once you've made a cut, everyone can serve themselves.'

Brona, with a sense of the dramatic, stood up, held the dagger over her head with both hands, then plunged it down into the side of the boar. Those sitting around the circle gave a great cheer and began to serve themselves amid talk and laughter.

After the meal, bonfires lit up the gathering darkness, and harpers began their songs. There were wooden harps that produced mellow music, and soft bodhráns to beat time when all those present sang ballads about ancient battles and the glories of former days. Datho's bard sang songs he had composed that day, praising his master's greatness in calling the contest, and his generosity in offering the bowl as a trophy. Then a visiting musician from outside the kingdom began to play on a harp of gold. It was so sweet that the company became entranced as they listened. When he stopped playing, silence remained over the gathering until he began again.

'Look,' Rory whispered to Róisín, pointing beyond the feasting nobles and their attendants to the dark fringes of the bonfires. 'We'll never see that sight again.'

Róisín glimpsed a ring of animals that had crept close, summoned by the sweet sound of the golden harp. There were squirrels, hedgehogs and foxes side by side with boars and badgers. Deer, the shyest of animals, were standing near a pack of wolves. On trees nearby, birds had risen from their nests to perch within earshot.

Still the harper played his magic harp. He picked up speed for the livelier tunes. People began to tap their feet and become animated again, and Rory and Róisín saw birds and animals slip away, back to the safety of their burrows, lairs and nests.

The listeners' thoughts returned to the present moment. The harper's tune invited them to dance. Round and round they whirled, full of joy. Other harpers plucked their harpstrings to join with the music of the golden harp. When all were in motion and other musicians played loudly, the golden harp became silent and its owner slipped away unnoticed. Later, people would wonder if they had imagined this magic sound.

When the festivities were at their height, the children met near where Samhain was sitting. He saw them and called them over. 'How are my favourite champions?' he asked them with a laugh.

'We're having a great time,' Aidan said.

'I was wondering where Lú had got to,' Róisín said. 'And is Archeld still with him?'

Samhain gave a huge roar of laughter. 'Archeld let him down this time,' he said. 'I wonder what punishment Lú might think up for an anti-druid whose spells don't work.'

'We're going to go back to the racecourse tomorrow, to look at the fiery chariot,' Rory said. 'I hope it will still be there in the morning.'

Samhain turned to Rory. 'I wouldn't mind seeing that myself,' he said. 'Why don't we all go now?'

The four looked at each other. 'Would we see much in the dark?' Róisín wondered aloud.

'We would if I bring torch-bearers,' Samhain assured them.

The four exchanged glances. Each of them knew the others wanted to go to see the chariot as badly as they did themselves. 'Right,' said Brona, 'what are we waiting for?'

Samhain organised torch-bearers from among his slaves and they set out for the racecourse. It was exciting to leave the bonfires and fiery glow of the feast and head into the pitch darkness, where the torches cast dancing shadows.

When they were almost there, Brona called softly to Samhain: 'Someone is there before us, master. Take care.'

Samhain, in the lead, marched across to where Brona had seen movement. 'Who is there?' he called. 'Answer Samhain, Datho's master silversmith.'

With a cry of despair, the crouching figure stood up, and in the torchlight Samhain recognised Cruachan, silversmith to Lord Lú of the North, who had once stolen Datho's Bowl.

'Cruachan!' exclaimed Samhain, standing in front of his former enemy with a taunting grin. 'Whoever gave you such a fearsome wound to your left cheek?'

The four looked at the result of the cruel gash they had seen Samhain inflict on Cruachan when he had fought him hand-to-hand back in the woods near his crannóg. The scar gave him a mean, twisted look.

'You know it was *you* who gave me the dreadful blow,' Cruachan answered. 'Are you not satisfied?'

Samhain stopped laughing at Cruachan. 'I am satisfied,' he said, 'and I admit that you fought like a man when I challenged you. You have paid for your theft. Should both of us not let past quarrels go now, eh? Master silversmiths should not remain enemies.'

Samhain held out his right arm. Cruachan gave him an arm-clasp, delighted to end the bad feeling between them. 'We are here tonight to see what is left of Lú's fiery chariot,' Samhain declared.

'I am trying to put it together now,' Cruachan said. 'Lú wants to bring it back north when we leave here. You are welcome to look.'

Samhain and the children crowded around the remains of the fiery chariot: blackened wood, spoiled decoration and damaged wheels. It looked as if the chariot had indeed been through fire but in some magical way had not been consumed.

'I can help you fix the wheels if you like,' Rory offered. 'It wouldn't take long to get it moving again.' Cruachan gladly accepted Rory's generous offer. Rory took off his cloak and fine jacket and handed them to Aidan to hold for him. He set to work with Cruachan, and in no time the broken wheels were mobile again. 'They're not perfect,' Rory said, 'but they should hold until you get home to Carragdove.'

Samhain and the four children then left Cruachan and returned to rejoin the feast. Music still sounded, nobles still danced, and mead still flowed plentifully. The children and Samhain made the most of it all. Soon the feast was at its loudest.

No one saw Archeld step from the shadows with his rowan wand to work his evil spell. Sleep came to everyone as suddenly as it had come to Magdawna. Everybody inside the fort, and all those outside at the feast, fell asleep where they were.

'Sleep will possess all of you until sunrise tomorrow,' Archeld said, grinning evilly.

# 11

## The Awakening

Róisín gazed around her. Why had daylight come so suddenly? She saw Brona and the boys pick up their silver drinking vessels from the ground with puzzled looks on their faces. How had silence descended so abruptly on the revellers?

People began to stand up and look around them. Róisín stood up too and called softly to the others: 'Look at Datho's table. Look at Maeve and Scathach.' The three others came to stand beside her before moving up near Maeve at the top table, where Datho was examining the dishes in front of him and berating his slaves for allowing the food to go cold.

Maeve was as mystified as Róisín. 'How can this food be cold already?' she asked her host. 'It is not two minutes since they placed it in front of us.'

Magdawna came over to his mother and placed his hand on her arm. 'Perhaps you should ask Scathach what has happened,' he said. 'This is how it was with me yesterday when I first woke from my enchanted sleep. I could not believe that any time had passed. I felt I had moved from one instant only as far as the next.'

Maeve looked horrified. 'You mean we have *all* been bewitched?'

Magdawna nodded his head solemnly. 'We know how

powerful Archeld is. If he could put *me* under such a spell, why could he not cast it over the whole company?'

At that moment, Scathach reached Maeve's side and bowed deeply before her. 'Forgive me, Majesty,' she said. 'Even had I known Archeld's intent, I would have been powerless to stop him. I was unable to break his spell over your son. He has authority that can sometimes be greater than mine.'

'No one is all-powerful, noble Scathach,' Maeve assured her arch-druidess. 'There have been many times and many ways in which you have protected us from him.'

Datho heard this exchange. His alert brown eyes had taken in the disarray of the whole scene. He was distressed that he was failing to provide for the needs of his guests, and had already given orders to clean up spillages, collect broken goblets and clear away cold food. Bewildered slaves, themselves confused by the turn of events, hastened to carry out his orders. Datho then turned to Maeve. 'Have you any idea, noble Maeve, why Archeld has done this?'

'Noble Datho, it is my opinion that he did it because he *could* do it. It was a nasty parting shot before he departed for Carragdove with his master,' she replied, her voice heavy with contempt for Lú's fearsome anti-druid.

'Could it be that he wished to allow Lú to depart unnoticed?' Scathach's dark eyes were thoughtful. 'Perhaps he feared that, had they known Lú was leaving, some competitor among those he injured on the track might seek revenge on Lú and on himself for the damage done to them.'

Datho looked up sharply at this suggestion. 'Would there be any other reason for Lú to hide his departure?' he said. 'Any reason we have not yet discovered or considered?'

Datho's slaves now appeared with hot food for breakfast. After they had eaten, the children went to their tents to put on their travelling clothes. Maeve, Ailill and Magdawna accompanied Datho into his palace, where attendants waited to ready them for their long trek back to Ardalba.

Wrapped in her travelling cloak, Maeve took a last look around her room. 'We haven't forgotten anything, have we?' she asked Ailill.

He looked around him. 'Our attendants have done a good job,' he answered. 'There is not so much as a gold bead left.' He put his hand out to Maeve to lead her out of the room.

The royal couple met Magdawna outside the bedroom, in his riding clothes once more. 'Mother,' Magdawna said, 'which of your slaves packed Datho's Bowl? I cannot see it with any of our people.'

Maeve turned deathly white. 'That's it,' she said. 'That's why Archeld bound us with a spell of deep sleep. It was to allow him to steal the bowl, and give Lú time to get far north with it before we noticed it was gone.'

Ailill led Maeve to an oak bench that stood against the wall of the passage. 'Perhaps you are mistaken, madam,' Ailill said. 'First I will check our bearers and question our attendants. I will return shortly.' While Maeve waited, her rage grew.

Ailill was soon back, this time looking almost as ashen as Maeve herself. 'Each one thought another had packed the bowl, madam,' he said. 'The truth is that there is no sign of it. I fear it is in Lú's possession.'

Everyone looked at the queen, waiting to see where her anger would strike. She stood up slowly, her features reddening, her deep-violet eyes glowing with rage. 'How dare Lú slight me thus,' she thundered. 'How dare he take what is justly mine, hard won in spite of his druid's spells. It is time he was taught not to meddle with Maeve of the Thousand Spears. By my moonstone, I will make him sorry for this deed. Now it is war. I will bring my armies to his gates. I myself will lead them. I will not only regain Datho's Bowl, I will seize his Brown Bull of Cooley and bring it west to Ardalba. That will make him a laughing stock throughout the land, and foolish in the eyes of his warriors.'

The children were impressed by the words of the warrior queen, but Ailill was shocked by his wife's speech. 'I implore you, madam, to be calm,' he pleaded. 'When you go to war with Lú you will need the alliance of every kingdom in the land of Erin, and much preparation besides. You are not ready now. Do not rush to disaster.'

'Husband,' shrieked Maeve, 'do not forget that *I* am mistress at Ardalba.'

'I do not forget,' Ailill retorted with spirit, 'but if you undertake this disastrous war, soon there will be no Ardalba for you to rule.'

'Would you have me take Lú's insult without protest?' Maeve asked him. 'Have you no pride in what Ardalba is, in what I have made it?'

Maeve made no attempt to keep her voice down. Datho came hurrying in, anxious to discover what the shouting was about. Ailill told him. Datho's face grew pale. 'No, noble Maeve,' he protested. 'I am your greatest ally and also your friend, and I tell you we are not yet ready for war.'

Many people beyond the hallway where the royal party stood heard the queen's voice raised in argument. Soon Maeve's own people, waiting outside the palace, informed several who had come from foreign lands about the theft of Datho's Bowl. This knowledge spread to others until it reached the ears of all who had run the race. Among those were Falga, Eric and Penardun.

Maeve's rage continued. She stamped her foot and shouted at all near her. She tore her cloak from her shoulder, its gold pin falling to the ground. Had Lú been present, she would have challenged him to single combat herself. This woman, who had champions to fight for her, needed none.

Meanwhile Falga, Eric and Penardun came together. Each looked at the other two and knew that they were thinking along the same lines. They could help Maeve recover her trophy, and at the same time make Lú pay for their own suffering at the hands of Archeld and his bewitched fiery chariot. They came to the palace and beckoned to Aidan to come outside with them. 'We would help your queen,' Falga said, speaking for all three of them. 'We will follow this evil king and his druid, and take the trophy back from him. But we do not know our way around your land. Can you lead us to his fort?'

Aidan thought for a moment. He certainly knew his way around better than when they had first come to Ardalba. And he was good at orienteering. He could find his way north, and then they could ask people when the king might have passed. 'I can guide you towards Lú's stronghold,' he said to the charioteers. 'The four of us can go with you, and between us we can recover Datho's Bowl.'

'Good,' said Eric. 'No one overturns my chariot and gets away with it.'

Maeve was still raging inside the fort when Aidan called the other three outside to tell them what he and the charioteers were planning. 'Good idea,' Rory said. 'Between us, we should be able to get the bowl back to Ardalba.' Róisín and Brona agreed. Rory made a signal to Ailill to come outside, and the children told him everything. All they needed now was to get Maeve to listen to reason.

In the end, it was Datho who persuaded the queen. When she had heard what the children had suggested, she was pleased to think that she might get her bowl back without a full-scale war, and more important, that Lú, and not herself, would be shamed before his peers. 'We must do this at once,' she said, taking charge again. 'Our only hope is to catch up with Lú before he reaches his stronghold at Carragdove. He has already had a start of several hours.'

Soon Ailill had arranged everything. The children would take Maeve's two racing chariots. Datho would lend three others, for Falga, Eric and Penardun, whose chariots had been destroyed in the race, and he would send a fighting man with each one. Maeve sent the guards the children had met the first day they arrived in Ardalba: Dian, son of Mog, and his friend Finian, with the squashed-looking face. Datho sent three slaves to take care of his chariots and those who rode in them. He lent his strongest horses to those slaves, and to the attendants and guards, who had no place in a chariot.

Before noon, the party was ready to leave Dara Mór. Maeve, Datho and all their nobles came out to wish the travellers success and a good journey. The chariots drove out in single file past the assembly. When they were approaching Maeve, the queen stopped the chariots to speak with the children. 'Thank you for going into danger for me yet again,' she said. 'I am glad that you offered to do this. It is so difficult a task that I would not have asked you to undertake it.'

'We are your high nobles, Majesty,' Róisín said. 'You honoured us when you named us Rescuers of the Realm. Are we not pledged to assist Ardalba?'

'Bring back the trophy,' Maeve said. The children were sure there were tears in her eyes. 'We will return to Ardalba and wait for you there.'

Magdawna stood with his mother. He arm-clasped the four children, bidding them safe journey. 'I will escort my mother and her people safely to the borders of Ardalba,' he said. 'Then I will follow your tracks to seek you out in the far north.'

The queen and her attendants stood back and allowed the cavalcade to set out north to seek Lú's black fortress at Carragdove. Aidan's chariot led the rest, his white horses full of energy and impatient to be gone. He would be the pathfinder in this quest for Datho's Bowl. None of the company had ever travelled so far north, or ventured into Lú's kingdom.

The chariots filed past Datho and Maeve. After a while, as Datho's stronghold grew smaller behind them, the children heard Samhain and his party sing the song they always sang when they left their crannóg. Soon all watching with them joined in the stirring chant, giving heart to those facing danger in the north in their daring attempt to recover Datho's Bowl.

# 12

## THE CHASE STARTS

Aidan led the party north. They were not exactly a war party, but he didn't know what else they could be called. He knew that Eric, Falga and Penardun were all prepared to face Lú in single combat, and that Datho's people and Maeve's two guards, Dian and Finian, would support them. Aidan wanted no part in violent confrontation, and he knew that Rory, Róisín and Brona would also prefer to recover the bowl without bloodshed. When they had travelled for an hour in a northerly direction, Aidan stopped to rest the horses and to get his bearings.

'How are you going to get us to Carragdove?' Rory asked when the four of them were able to talk privately. 'We've never been there before, and there aren't any roads or signposts.'

'North is easy to find,' Aidan replied. 'All we need is sight of the sun now and then, and to see the stars at night.'

'Even so,' Brona said, 'you could go north and miss Lú's stronghold altogether. All Datho told us is that Carragdove is on the northern seaboard and that the route to it passes along by the western shore of a great lake.'

'We're still in Ireland, aren't we?' said Aidan. 'So what big lake can be found north-east of where we are now?'

'That would be Lough Neagh,' Róisín said, remembering her map.

'Of course it is,' Aidan agreed. 'And what size is Lough Neagh?'

'It's enormous,' Róisín said, 'like an inland sea.'

'If we follow a line a bit to the east of north,' Aidan said, 'I can't see how we can miss that huge body of water.'

Before continuing their journey, Aidan realigned their route using the sun. The other travellers were impressed by his actions, thinking he used magic power from the sun to direct them.

The day wore on, with travelling broken only by short stops. Eventually, everyone realised that they would not catch up with Lú before nightfall. They decided to go as far as they could in the failing light before pitching camp for the night. They lay under cloudy skies, wrapped in their cloaks, to sleep the sleep of travel-weary people.

At daybreak, they set out once more, going as fast as their horses could manage. Soon they were glad they had decided not to travel on the previous evening. They came to a large tract of bog land which was waterlogged, and the chariot wheels got stuck. It was a desolate spot where in the dark they could easily have fallen into deep bog holes and been heard of no more. They led their horses with head-ropes, creeping forward step by step. Aidan found few landmarks to establish a line to lead him north. 'Noble Aidan, look!' Eric, who was much taller than anyone else, pointed ahead. 'A road,' he said. 'A causeway through the bog.'

Soon they could all see it. Before long they were safely on it and could use their chariots again. This road was built up slightly above the general level of the bog, and was surfaced with tree trunks laid across the road from side to side. Between each tree trunk and the next, earth and stones had been used to fill up the gaps. It gave a bumpy ride but was safe and solid.

'It took a lot of people to build this road,' Brona remarked, 'and a lot of hard work.'

'I expect Lú has crossed here before us,' Rory said, 'but I can't see any wheel-tracks.'

The trunk road continued for a couple of miles. Where it stopped, the bog was dry once more. The party continued until the bog land lay behind them. 'Noble Aidan,' Eric called to Aidan, in the leading chariot, 'there are dwellings ahead.' Aidan stepped down from his chariot to lead his horses, making signs to everyone else to move quietly. Before long, they could all see the dwellings. They were circular huts thatched with straw, scattered over a shallow hillside.

Falga and Penardun both left Datho's fighting men in charge of their chariots to stand beside Aidan. 'These people may be hostile,' they warned. 'We are not yet in Lú's kingdom. These will be suspicious border folk.'

The party, still led by Aidan, continued to where their way would take them past these dwellings, without moving between them. Soon they saw people gathering to observe them. Before long, a spokesman, with a spear in each hand, approached them. 'Who be ye, and what be your business?' he asked bluntly.

'We come from Datho, Lord of the East,' Aidan replied, as he was at the front of the group. 'Some of us are in his service. We seek Lú, Lord of the North, and would ask you how long ago he passed through here.'

'We do not assist strangers,' the man told them, 'although we are neither for Lú nor against him. Now I warn you that you should move on and delay no longer in this place. Be gone before nightfall.'

Aidan heard Falga rattle his sword behind him. 'Is that how you speak to noble Aidan of the court of Maeve of the Thousand Spears?' Falga demanded.

'I speak civilly,' the man replied, 'and my message is clear. Be gone before harm befalls you.'

With that, he turned away from them to return to where the other border folk waited. 'It might be the best thing if we did move on,' said Rory, 'at least until we are out of sight of these unfriendly people.'

'You're probably right,' Róisín agreed, 'but it is already late afternoon. We need to find a safe camping ground. We don't want to be caught unprepared at nightfall.'

Penardun came up from his place in the cavalcade. 'If we get moving right away,' he said, 'we should be able to reach the other side of that little hill before dark.' He pointed to it with his spear. 'They won't be too sure where we are then.'

'That's a good plan,' Aidan said. 'Are we ready to move forward?' All the chariots set off again behind Aidan's. Those on horseback brought up the rear. In no time, they were making good speed across land that grew steadily stonier.

'Stop!' They heard a sudden shout from Falga, and pulled up the horses to see what the matter was. Falga stood beside his chariot looking at his left wheel. 'Two spokes suddenly snapped,' he said. 'I can go no further until they are mended.'

'Well, that settles where we spend the night,' Róisín said. 'Do you think you can repair it before dark?'

'I might be able to do it,' Falga replied. 'I'll get started right away.'

Rory, who had repaired the spokes on the fiery chariot, offered to help. While he and Falga worked on the wheel, some of the party began to prepare hot food, while others kept lookout. Falga and Rory improvised hammers from heavy stones, used knives to carve wood to the shapes they needed, and twisted grass into strong cord to bind their repairs firmly to the wheel frame.

While they worked, a slave-girl crept over from the settlement, so furtively that watching border folk failed to see her leave. She would have been pretty, with her brown hair and green eyes, if she had not looked as if she had been starved for weeks. Her ragged slave's tunic and cloak were in tatters, and hung loosely on her thin frame. She saw Aidan first and came up to speak to him, thinking he was the leader of the party. 'Master,' she said, bowing low, 'I heard border folk talking. I heard them say you asked about Lord Lú of the North. They decided to tell you nothing, but now I bring you word of Lord Lú. He passed this way at first light, and is ahead of you by almost a full day.'

Eric, who was beside Aidan, looked with suspicion at the girl. 'Why do you help us against the wishes and practice of your people?' he demanded.

The girl continued to speak to Aidan. 'These are not my people, master. They stole me from my home in the far north-west and have made me their slave. Please let me travel with you until I reach my homeland once again.'

Róisín had been standing nearby during this exchange. 'We'll never catch Lú before he reaches Carragdove,' she said. 'Not if he's a whole day ahead of us.'

'We'll give it a good try, though,' Aidan said. 'Maybe *he*'ll crack a wheel or two along the way, and we'll be able to catch up with him.' He turned to the slave girl, who was still bowing humbly before him. 'What is your name?' he asked her.

'My name is Sive,' she replied. 'I am from the family of Ronan. My father is the leader of our people, and a skilled craftsman, a master chariot-maker. Our crannóg is the largest on our part of our river.'

'I am Aidan,' he said, 'and I am not master here. We will discuss between all of us whether to take you with us or not. Then we will tell you what we decide.'

'There is more, noble Aidan,' the slave-girl continued. 'The border folk plan to attack you at nightfall. They often attack travellers at night, to steal their riches, their animals, and even their children, as they did me.'

When he heard this, Aidan called everyone together except Falga and Rory, who were busy mending the broken wheel. After they had heard Sive's news, the others agreed that she could travel with them for her own safety. No one wanted her to return to the border folk, where she would be severely punished or even killed if they found out that she had helped them.

Sive could not express how grateful she was to them. 'Thank you,' she said again and again, between bouts of laughing and crying, until Róisín took charge of her and convinced her that she was safe now. 'Or at least as safe as any of us are,' Róisín added. 'And don't worry, we should be able to bring you close to where your home is. You'll be free for good once you get there.'

'What about the attack by the border folk?' Brona asked them all. 'What should we do about that?'

'I suggest that we behave as if we did intend to camp here overnight,' Penardun said. 'Keep the horses harnessed for the road, and then, when they start an attack, with luck Falga's chariot will be ready, and we can drive swiftly away from them.'

Meanwhile, as the sun slipped down in the sky, Rory and Falga worked as quickly as they could. 'We have to get things right the first time,' Rory said. 'There won't be a chance to do anything twice.' They shaped wood with their knives, carving it as best they could into the shape of the other spokes. They bound the wheel strongly at its weak points. Finally, they fixed the two new spokes to the wheel-frame. The wheel they had mended looked perfect. But would it take the chariot's weight, and would it be strong enough to withstand the vibrations when the chariot reached rough ground?

'Let's put the wheel back on its axle,' Rory suggested. 'When we know it will take the chariot's weight, let's get into it one by one, as many as can fit standing in it at one time. Then we can all jump up and down in it. If it survives that, we'll just have to trust that it will travel without breaking again, even where the ground is rough.'

Out of sight of the border folk, they began to test the wheel. When they put the axle in the wheel, Rory held his breath. The new spokes remained firm. Then he stepped into the chariot. The spokes still held. Then Falga got in. Then two slaves stepped up, followed by Penardun, when he saw what they were doing. The spokes stayed in place. 'Now let's all jump together,' Rory said. 'One, two, three!' They all jumped on the chariot floor. 'I think it's all right,' Rory said, delighted with their work. 'I think we've done it.'

'I think we have,' Falga agreed, grinning widely. 'If you ever need a job repairing chariots, come to Man. I'll make you my chief assistant.'

Just then, a slave on lookout duty called across softly. 'I see border folk moving,' he said. Everyone stopped to look across at the hillside. They saw the stealthy movements of men creeping towards them.

'Are we all ready?' Aidan whispered.

'Yes,' the others replied, also in a whisper.

The horses were already harnessed and waiting, and everyone knew what to do. When the first dweller was less than a spear's throw away, Aidan shook the reins to get his horses moving, and everyone followed him. Shouting loudly to frighten the border folk, everyone in the party got their horses to go as fast as possible. Soon they were strung out in a fast-moving line, leaving the attacking border folk far behind them.

'That was close,' Róisín said later, when they had found a safe place to stop for the night. 'If Sive hadn't warned us, goodness knows what would have happened.'

Sive blushed with embarrassment. 'I was pleased to help,' she said. 'Without all of you, I could have remained a slave of the border folk for life.'

'We'll take care of you now,' Róisín said. 'We'll get you home safely, we promise.'

Then they all got ready to settle down for the night. Under clear skies, the four children gazed into the heavens and marvelled at the brightness and number of the stars. They never saw that many back home in Glenelk, because of the street lights. Wrapped in their cloaks, one by one they fell asleep.

# 13

## EMANIA

Next morning, when the sun had risen bright and clear, Aidan decided on the route they should take. 'We should come to the Great Hill Fort of the North soon,' he said to the others. 'Lú will make for his stronghold of Carragdove, I am almost certain. But in case he should decide to shelter at the fort, we need to look out for signs of his presence.'

'I have heard of this great fort,' Penardun said. 'In the Land of Dragons we call it Emania. It is a famous seat of druidic power and culture.'

'What signs exactly should we look for, to tell us that Lú is there?' Eric asked.

'Lú was crowned King of the North at Emania,' Róisín said. 'His standard would be raised inside the fort. You saw it on his chariot at the race – it's red, with a large black hand embroidered across it.'

Once they had got everybody moving, the children decided to keep going until the horses needed to rest. Soon a tall mountain took shape ahead of them; it seemed to grow higher the nearer they came to it. Before long they could see the outline of the Great Hill Fort of the North stretching across its summit. No one had expected Emania to be so big.

'Are we going to climb up there?' Rory asked Aidan.

'Some of us are,' Aidan replied. 'Anyone who doesn't want to go up to the fort can wait at the bottom with the chariots and horses.'

They continued on in the strong midday heat until the chariots could go no further up the steep ground, and both horses and people needed a break. Here they stopped and made camp. 'Who's going to go up to the fort then?' Rory asked.

There was a short silence while the children looked at each other. None of them wanted to miss out on seeing Emania, knowing that in their own era nothing remained of it except outlines of its boundaries. 'Let's *all* go,' Róisín suggested.

When it was clear that all four children wanted to climb to the fort, Eric, Penardun and Falga offered to go with them for protection. The children were glad the warriors would join them. The rest of the party remained with the chariots and horses.

'Wait for us,' Róisín told all those who were staying at the camp, 'no matter how long we are. If we are not back by nightfall, prepare to sleep here. We do not know how we may be delayed.'

What was clear at once to the climbing party was that Emania was a busy place. Many people approached it or left it on horseback or on foot, using well-trodden paths to the summit. Aidan soon directed them to the left, where they joined one of these paths.

'It would be better if we could discover whether Lú is here *before* we get as far as the entrance,' Rory said.

'There's an easy way to do that,' Brona answered. 'Leave it to me.'

She had seen, far ahead, two slaves coming down the path towards them. Whatever their business, these slaves would surely know whether Lú was at the fort or not. When they came within hailing distance, she shouted up to them: 'We come from the Lord of the East. Can you tell us if Lord Lú has returned to his fort yet?'

'You've missed him,' one of the slaves answered. 'He passed here yesterday, bound for Carragdove, his black fortress in the far north. You will not overtake him before he reaches it. He drove as if demons chased him.'

Brona thanked the slaves and wished them a good journey. When the slaves had passed on, the four children discussed with Falga, Eric and Penardun what they should do now. For one thing, they would not be able to catch up with Lú before he got to his stronghold. Meanwhile, Emania towered above them. They couldn't bear to leave without seeing what it was like inside.

Róisín, who had always loved history, remembered reading about the ancient laws of hospitality. 'Do you know what I've just remembered?' she said to the others. 'At major royal residences like this, the lord or his steward was under obligation to give food and lodging to visitors. If we go up and tell the steward we are looking for Lord Lú, he will have to offer us this hospitality, and we will have a chance to look around inside. It's too late in the day for him to turn us away. What do you think?'

Brona, Aidan and Rory thought about it for a few seconds. Then, at the same time, they all said, 'Let's go for it.' The children explained to Falga and the others what they planned to do.

The men were delighted with the plan. 'In our own lands,' Eric said, 'Emania is renowned as a place of might and culture. Now I alone, of all my people, will be able to say I have seen it.'

With everything decided, all seven of them set out once more to climb the rest of the way to the fort. The nearer they got to it, the more impressive the fort became. Who could breach its defences or climb its lofty banks unchallenged? Up and up they went, higher and higher still, until they came to level ground outside the towering earthen bank that protected it. Ahead of them at the entrance stood great gates of wood and bronze, almost as high as the bank itself. By day, the gates were open to those who came and went about their business.

As the children and their escorts were walking in, a duty guard at the inner ditch challenged them. 'State your names,' he demanded, 'and the purpose of your visit.'

'We are high nobles,' Aidan said. 'We travel from Datho, Lord of the East. We have business with Lord Lú of Emania.' He gave their names, and those of the charioteers.

The guard bowed to them. 'Pray wait,' he said, 'until I fetch Morna, Steward of the North, to welcome you in a fitting manner.'

They were all within the massive defences now, and could look around inside the large enclosure of the fort. Straight in front of them, in the centre of the huge complex, stood two enormous circular buildings that seemed to touch each other. 'Look!' Rory pointed to open ground on their left. 'They're playing hurling.'

Teams of youths in their late teens were indeed playing a game that looked like hurling, which they had often watched at home. The noise their sticks made when they struck against each other reminded them of the clash of the ash.

Róisín had been thinking of her history book again. 'Do you think Cúchulainn might play there?' she asked. 'This is where he lived and trained.'

'*Someone*'s training over there,' said Aidan, pointing to their right. Youths who looked like young warriors were practising with slingshots, while others threw spears at targets. 'Are they training for war?' he asked.

'They must be Red Branch champions,' Róisín said, with awe in her voice, 'or at least men training to become champions.'

Brona laughed. 'Lú will need all the Red Branch champions he can find when Maeve decides to capture his Brown Bull of Cooley.'

They saw the steward coming towards them from the buildings, and said no more about Maeve, knowing that Lú regarded her as his enemy. The steward was clearly a man of power and authority. He strode confidently towards them. 'Welcome to Emania,' he called as he drew near. 'I am Morna. I greet you in the name of my master, Lú, and pray you will accept our hospitality until morning.'

Róisín, as a high noble, answered him. 'We accept your hospitality tonight, master steward, and thank you for it. Morning light must see us on our way.'

Morna conducted them towards the building on the left. This was the king's palace, he told them. The palace on their right, which was almost as grand, was the centre of druidic power and study. 'At Emania, we train soldiers for the king,' he told them. 'And here too, student druids train. They are apprenticed to master druids in other centres here and abroad for seventeen years before becoming full druids.'

The children exchanged discreet glances. None of them could ever forget Ulcas Spellbinder, who was apprenticed to Archeld, Lú's anti-druid. Was he or Archeld in Emania at that moment?

Rory decided to find out whether Ulcas was there. 'We have heard of the great Archeld,' he told Morna. 'People say he always travels with Lord Lú.'

'Indeed he does,' Morna confirmed. 'Lú needs him with him at all times.'

'And we have met Ulcas Spellbinder, his pupil,' Rory

added. 'Is he still on his island in the Lake of Tranquil Swans?'

'Indeed he is,' Morna replied. 'He is almost a full druid now. He will return here next year but will stay only for his inauguration ceremony.'

The children felt safer knowing that these old enemies of theirs would not trouble them today at Emania.

'Do you wish to walk around the fort before we enter the palace?' Morna asked them. 'I can send an attendant to guide you.'

The three charioteers were as anxious as the children to see everything Emania had to offer. Falga answered the steward: 'I, and the people of Man, have heard tell of Emania and its splendour. I would wish to be able to describe it fully when I return to my homeland.'

Morna summoned an attendant to show them around the fort. The attendant was slim but not tall. Her bronze skin and jet-black hair marked her as a captive. Her dark, lustrous eyes looked sad. She bowed to them, and spoke in gentle tones. 'My name is Naomi. We will go anywhere you wish within the fort except the druids' academy.'

For the next hour, they followed Naomi all over the enclosure. A game was still in progress on the playing field. 'Our trainee warriors need to develop strength and endurance,' Naomi told the visitors. 'They also learn to run for many miles, to leap over high obstacles, to swim through flooded rivers, to lift heavy weights, and to develop strength and accuracy with the slingshot and spear. They prepare for single combat by learning how to use a sword skilfully.'

The fort was larger than Maeve's stronghold at Ardalba but had the same main features. There was an animal enclosure and a cooking area, and some small circular dwellings, perhaps the homes of slaves. And there was the second palace, the seat of druidism, into which they could not go.

'What do druids study?' Rory asked.

'They study healing and the use of herbs,' Naomi said. 'They learn about the seasons and the stars. They understand philtres and potions, and can use them either to harm or to help. They have knowledge of the past. As priests, they approach the gods to appease their wrath. Their power is beyond that of kings.'

Rory was surprised at this. He thought druids would study spells and how to make trouble for people when their master demanded it. He had not expected them to have such wisdom.

Naomi conducted the visitors back to the king's palace, where seven other attendants waited for them. These attendants brought them to rooms that were larger and more magnificent than those they had used at Ardalba. Slaves were preparing baths for them. They saw that the bathwater was being heated by stones taken from large braziers in which fires burned to warm their rooms.

Once again they were dressed as high nobles, their travelling clothes taken away for cleaning. Róisín and Brona were lent court garments in which red and black were the dominant colours, while the boys and charioteers wore red cloaks ornamented with Lú's Black Hand icon. It seemed to be the custom at Emania that guests should wear Lú's colours while they were at his fort. Gold hair-ornaments and brooches were also part of their dress, and both girls had necklaces of jet and silver beads.

Attendants conducted them to the great hall, where the feasting was about to begin. Intricate bronze horns were blown to herald each dish, as slaves carried them in and laid them before Morna and his many guests. The food was more lavish and plentiful than they had yet seen on their travels, except at Datho's feast after the chariot race. There was little talk while they ate. When all were satisfied, the music and storytelling began. Emania's bards were famed throughout the land. They praised Lú for his constant readiness for war and for his swordsmanship and skill with the slingshot. It seemed that being warlike was the only thing for which Lú was highly regarded among his people.

As soon as they could, the four children departed for their rooms, claiming tiredness after their journey. 'We leave at first light tomorrow, right?' Rory couldn't wait to continue their search for Lú and for Datho's Bowl.

'They'll open the gates at daybreak, I suppose,' Róisín said. 'Let's be ready to go the minute they do.'

'What about Morna?' Brona asked. 'He treated us well. Shouldn't we say goodbye to him?'

'That's a good idea,' Aidan agreed. 'If we leave without following the custom by saying farewell, he might begin to suspect us. We don't want a band of Red Branch champions sent after us, do we?'

So the next morning, all seven of them waited until Morna was free to meet them. They then thanked him for his hospitality, telling him that they must be on their way. 'You have shown us great kindness,' Rory said. 'Lord Datho will appreciate the honour you have bestowed on us.' Morna gave each of them a friendly arm-clasp and wished them a safe journey. He stood to watch them until they had reached the gates. Here they bowed to him and waved a final salute, which Morna acknowledged before he turned and went back into the fort.

# 14

## To Carragdove

From the high gates of Emania, the valley below them seemed distant, its details hidden. Children and charioteers set out for the long trek down to where they had left their horses and attendants. 'What a place!' Falga exclaimed, turning back to take a last look at the fort's lofty banks. 'Lú's druid cheated me of a chance to win in Datho's contest. The memories of my visit to Emania and the hospitality offered to me there are worth more than any trophy.'

'I agree,' Eric said. 'My memory of my night at this great hill fort will never leave me.'

'You are both right,' Penardun declared, 'but for myself, I would have preferred to bring Datho's Bowl back to the Land of Dragons. When I return there, I must now admit defeat – I who never suffered it before.'

The four children felt sorry for these brave men who had come so far to represent their people in Datho's great contest, only to be beaten by such trickery. Who knows, Aidan thought, if there had been no fiery chariot, would Brona really have won the race?

That was the last time any of them looked back at Emania. They travelled down to the plain, until they could make out where their chariots were grouped in the shadow of the mountain. Their attendants saw them coming and rushed out to wait for them. One tall figure stepped away from the rest and began to climb up to meet them. 'Look!' Róisín called to the others. 'It's Magdawna. He's come to join us.'

They began to run the rest of the way to meet him, with Róisín in front of the others. 'Noble Magdawna,' she called, panting, 'we did not expect to see you so soon.'

'Noble Róisín,' Magdawna replied, greeting her with a firm arm-clasp, 'I escorted my father and mother with their party to the borders of our land. When they were safely there, they gave me permission to follow you as I had promised, and to assist you in recovering Datho's Bowl from Lú. I have hastened to catch up with you.'

Soon they were all back at the camp. Magdawna was pleased to meet Falga, Eric and Penardun again. When they had exchanged all the news about their journeys, Magdawna went to talk to Sive. When she told him about her life as a slave among the border folk, he promised that they would not leave her until they had returned her to her people. 'That much I guarantee,' he said, 'but first we must pursue Lú to Carragdove and recover the stolen trophy.'

'My family lives far west of Mermaid's House Lake,' Sive said, 'at a place on a river where two other large lakes almost meet. My father is a famous craftsman. He makes chariots – beautiful ones bound with bronze and silver.'

'We will find him for you,' Magdawna assured her. 'Meanwhile, you will travel as one of us. Your slave days are over for ever.' Sive was so happy that she did not stop smiling all day.

Now it was time for them to set out again for Carragdove. The attendants harnessed the horses to the chariots. Slaves packed up their cooking pots and weapons, making sure that nothing was left behind. Magdawna had come from Ardalba on horseback. He decided that he would continue the journey with Aidan, who was still driving the lead chariot. 'Do you know which way to go from here?' Magdawna asked him.

'We go north until we reach Mermaid's House Lake, and then continue along by its western shore,' Aidan said. 'After that, I can find where north is by the sun and stars. The northern sea touches Carragdove.'

By afternoon, they saw the lake ahead of them, blue and shimmering in the late sunshine, and by the evening they were there, ready to make camp on a sandy beach, where the gentle lapping of waves would later lull them to sleep. 'All we have to do now,' Aidan told the others, 'is to keep the lake on our right and head north.'

Both the people and the horses were tired after their long trek. Slaves prepared salmon and trout they had caught in the lake. The children thought the fish was delicious, especially eaten under the stars.

'Do you see that very bright one?' Róisín asked the other children when no one else was near enough to hear. 'That's Jupiter. Do people know about planets in this era? Planets don't behave like stars. They must puzzle the druids.'

When the meal was over, they sat around the fire singing and telling tales. The children heard the storyteller tell the tale of little Princess Liban, whose house was drowned beneath the waters of the lake. One day the person guarding a well left the door to it unlocked. Spring-water overflowed through the door, and out on to the plain where Liban's house was built, until it covered the house completely. Everything else around it on the plain was submerged. All the people were drowned except Liban herself. She lived under water for a long time with her little dog, until the dog died. Then she turned into a mermaid and swam the seven seas for three hundred years.

'She may be swimming there yet,' the storyteller said,

finishing his tale. 'They say that if you take a coracle out across the waters of the lake, you can see her house far beneath you.' Brona sighed with satisfaction. What a lovely story, she thought.

*

The next morning, everybody felt keen to get on the road again. That day they saw many crannógs built out over the lake, and isolated dwellings of wattle and straw like those of the fisherfolk on Samhain's lakeside. These people made pottery drinking vessels and large containers for storing grain.

Before leaving the lakeside, they saw a few more isolated dwellings. A man came towards them from the nearest one and spoke to Magdawna in the leading chariot. 'Noble lord,' he said, 'please be watchful. There are robbers in your path who attack unsuspecting travellers. Your lives would not be safe from them if you were caught unawares.'

Magdawna was grateful for this warning. He gave the man a gift of a short dagger with an iron blade, which he took from a small scabbard attached to his sword scabbard. 'Thank you for alerting us,' he said. 'May all you do prosper.'

When the man had returned to his house, Magdawna gave new orders to all the attendants, particularly to Dian and Finian, Maeve's guards from Ardalba. They were to be extra watchful until the party had left danger behind them. 'If they attack us, will you fight beside me?' Magdawna asked Falga, Eric and Penardun. The warriors promised to do their best to see the robbers off. 'And now for you,' Magdawna said to the four children. 'If there is fighting, keep well back and we will protect you. My mother would not wish you harmed. You are too important to Ardalba.'

'What about Sive?' Brona asked.

'We can protect Sive too,' he answered.

'There is no need for that, noble lord,' Sive said. 'Women of Ronan's household always fight beside their men. I can strike someone with a slingshot or bring him down with a spear as neatly as any warrior.'

Magdawna looked at her in surprise. 'You don't look like a fighter,' he said, 'but if you wish to fight with us, we will be glad of your help.'

They continued on their journey, their senses sharpened to hear every sound and see every movement that might spell danger. In spite of their vigilance, robbers fell on them when they were about to resume their journey after their midday break for food. With loud shouts, six men jumped at them from behind great tree trunks. Their hair was long and wild and they were dressed in tattered animal skins. At once, guards and charioteers rallied round Magdawna, and each of the children found an attendant beside them to protect them, as Maeve's son had promised.

It was a fierce battle. Magdawna swung his great sword around him, and woe to the robber who stood in its way. The charioteers with Dian and Finian used spears to fight off the rough thieves. The robbers themselves roared and shouted, as if sound alone could defeat Magdawna's party.

'What can *we* do?' Róisín said desperately. 'We have to help them.'

'Let's sing Samhain's song,' Rory shouted, 'the one they sing when they are crossing the lake.'

'Good idea,' Brona agreed, and they all started to sing the song, hoping to frighten their enemies away.

Where had Sive been all this time? No one had had time to think about her. Then suddenly the robber who was trying to overcome Magdawna fell to the ground without a sound. After another minute, the robber grappling with Eric also fell.

The four children were still singing loudly when Aidan happened to look up. There, from her seat in the branches above their heads, Sive was aiming a slingshot at the robbers. It hit Falga's attacker. With three robbers down, the chant of the children seemed louder and louder. Suddenly, the remaining robbers broke loose and ran away.

Magdawna instructed Dian to tie up the fallen thieves. 'They won't be there long,' he said. 'The others will come back for them. We need time to escape from here with no one following us.'

Aidan drove the leading chariot away from the place of attack while Magdawna sorted out his weapons. 'I don't know what happened to the man I was fighting,' the prince said. '*I* didn't knock him down. He just seemed to fall.'

'It was Sive,' Aidan said. 'She's deadly with the slingshot. She got Eric's man as well, and Falga's.'

Magdawna laughed. 'Really? We could do with more like her.'

Next time they halted for rest, Magdawna thanked Sive for her help. 'You were our secret weapon, and a complete surprise for our attackers,' he said.

Later that afternoon, Rory suddenly stopped. 'What can I smell?' he asked, wrinkling his nose.

'That's the sea,' Brona said. 'We're nearly there. Carragdove can't be far off.'

Aidan and Magdawna urged their horses on. The others followed. To begin with, they could see little because there were trees on either side of them. But in a little while they were free of trees and out into open ground. And there ahead of them was the fort of Carragdove, built halfway up a mountainside, as Ardalba was.

Inside the stockade, they saw Lú's stronghold of blackest basalt towering over the circular buildings clustered around it. This was where Lú was lurking with his anti-druid, Archeld, and Datho's Bowl. The travellers saw guards at every entrance. How would they penetrate the fort's defences and recover the priceless trophy?

# 15

## LÚ'S BLACK FORTRESS

Magdawna decided to pitch camp. No one from the fort could
see them from that distance. 'After we've eaten, we'll think
about what to do,' he said.

Brona slipped away from the others to where no one could
watch her. She felt it was up to her to get the trophy back.
She had won it, and in a sense it was hers. She stood beneath
a great oak tree and concentrated on Pooka. *Help me, Pooka,*
she said in her mind. *I will need to be invisible to go into Lú's
palace to regain my trophy.* Brona waited with her eyes closed,
seeing Pooka as she had first seen him, the Wild Horse of
the Mountain, breathing fire from his nostrils.

Soon she heard his voice whispering in her ear. *I will
keep my promise, Brona,* he said, *but it is not for Róisín, Aidan
or Rory to know. It will be our secret.*

*When the moment comes, what should I do?* she asked.

*When that time comes, you must be alone,* he replied, *as
you must be alone when you wish to become visible again. To
call me, do what you have done today. Go to a place where no
one can see you. Close your eyes and summon me. Say, 'Pooka,
hide me from mortal sight.' Then you, your clothing, and anything
you hold will become invisible. When you wish to cast aside this
cloak of invisibility, call me again. Say, 'Pooka, reveal me to*

*mortal sight.' Then you and what you carry will be visible to everyone once more.*

When Brona returned to the camp, the food was ready. Everyone had a hearty appetite. The slaves had made a stew from small birds they had snared, and had baked hedgehogs in the fire.

After the meal, Magdawna called them together to discuss how they might best get into Lú's well-guarded fort and then get out again with Datho's Bowl. 'It is up to me alone to get the bowl back,' Brona announced with authority. 'I won it in the first place. Now I must rescue it and return it to Ardalba. I am still queen's champion, and wear Maeve's medal. Therefore it is my task, and mine only, to enter Carragdove to seek out the bowl.'

'My mother wishes all four of you to be protected from danger,' Magdawna said. 'How can I let you go into that fort alone?'

'He's right,' Aidan said. 'You'd be mad to go in by yourself.'

'Let me come with you,' Róisín offered. 'At least I could come back for help if you were caught.'

'I'm not going to be caught,' Brona said confidently. 'You can all stop worrying.'

'How can we not worry?' Rory asked her. 'If Lú or Archeld, or Fiachart himself, laid hands on you, they could do anything, even kill you.'

'I do not need help from mortals to protect me against mortals.' Brona stood up and suddenly seemed taller than before. She stared ahead, her dark-brown eyes fixed on the distant landscape. 'I am in tune with the Otherworld. I can summon help from there.'

Róisín, Rory and Aidan were stunned into silence. They remembered how Scathach had thought that Brona would make a good druid. They recalled how easily she had communicated with the Black Bull, and Elk and Badger. It was Brona who had undone the spell of forgetfulness that Ulcas Spellbinder had cast over them. And why had *she* not been blinded like the other contestants during the chariot race? They suddenly realized that Brona was more in tune than any of them with this strange world in which they found themselves, and with the mystical people and animals who lived beyond its fringes. Rory looked at Brona with new respect. 'I think she really could do it,' he said to the prince. 'I don't think she needs us at all.'

Reluctantly, Magdawna let himself be persuaded to allow Brona to go in alone. 'We will watch you climb to the fort,' he said. 'We will follow if we see a threat.'

Brona understood that he expected her to wait until morning. But she needed to be alone before she could ask Pooka to make her invisible: she could not have Magdawna and half the camp watching her. She decided to enter Carragdove later the same evening, when Lú's household would be feasting and feeling safe because they had reached their strong fort ahead of their pursuers.

As darkness approached, there was storytelling and laughter at Magdawna's camp. Brona took her chance to set out alone for Carragdove. Well away from the camp, she walked through a small copse that sheltered her from view. Here she sent out her thoughts to Pooka, saying, *Pooka, hide me from mortal sight*.

Brona felt nothing and heard nothing. She looked down at her hands. They were still there. She could see her clothes. She picked up a piece of fallen branch: she could see it. Nothing had disappeared. What was she to do? Had Pooka not heard her call? While Brona was wondering what to do, she saw a fox scuffling in her direction. He seemed to be heading straight towards her, his nose to the ground. Brona loved all animals. She waited to see how near he would come to her. Before she could stop him, he ran right into her, striking his nose against her leg. Terrified, he backed off, howling and snarling, rubbing his nose with his paw. Brona knew then that the fox had not seen her: she was invisible.

Brona strode confidently up the hill, knowing that Pooka would keep her invisible until she asked him to make her visible again. The guards on duty at the fort gate seemed bored, Brona thought. They were playing a game that looked a bit like chess. Would Lú approve of guards playing games when they were supposed to be on watch, Brona wondered. She walked straight through the large black gates, pausing to move one of the pieces on the playing board. At once, one of the guards accused the other of cheating. 'How could I have cheated?' the other guard replied. 'You saw my hands weren't near the board.'

Brona left them arguing. With each passing moment, she felt more confident that she would be able to rescue the bowl. Invisibility gave greater protection than any weapon. She heard shouting and loud laughter coming from the great hall, where the feasting had started at sundown. Brona guessed that that was where Datho's Bowl was on display. Not only would Lú boast about how he had got it, and lie by claiming that Fiachart had won it fairly in the race, but he would feel safer keeping it in his sight.

Brona continued further into the black palace, where red and black tapestries hung across openings to various rooms. The whole place was gloomy and dark, unlike the other palaces she had visited. She saw slaves carrying dishes in and out of the banquet hall, and followed them right into the heart of Lú's stronghold.

When Brona entered the hall, the feasting was at its height. Lú's bard was getting ready to sing – no doubt a special song about the great victory Lú had achieved in winning the precious trophy. The harper was tuning his harp with sharp twangs. Slaves were busy refilling jewelled drinking vessels with strong mead. Brona could see that everyone was already merry after drinking the mead.

She saw Lú sitting at his table of judgement. In front of him, on a piece of gold-embroidered cloth, sat Datho's Bowl. Its polished silver reflected the red firelight from the brazier of turf burning in the centre of the room.

Fiachart, his champion, had the honour of sitting on Lú's right hand, for bringing the bowl to the north. Lú could not admit to theft, and his arch-druid Archeld, who had stolen the bowl for him, could not be publicly honoured for his deed. Lú's queen, Eriú, sat on his left. Her full-length gown was deep crimson, and had long sleeves and wide cuffs, decorated with Celtic spirals embroidered in silver thread, and she was wearing a rich black cloak. Her light-gold hair was elaborately braided and tied, and her gold jewellery was heavy and elaborate, as befitted the wife of a powerful king.

From the doorway, Brona looked again at the bowl. She knew it was heavy. How was she to pick it up and walk out of the hall with it? Once she had picked it up, it would become invisible, but if she had to put it down, it would become visible again. Before walking into the hall, Brona took off her heavy cloak, which hung to the ground, and draped it over her arm. Her only chance to carry the bowl safely was to wrap it in this cloak. She could hold the four corners of the cloak so that it was like a giant cloth bag, with the bowl inside.

Brona slung the cloak over her arm and began to approach Lú's table through a crowd of slaves and attendants. Although she was being as careful as she could, the end of her cloak brushed across the bare legs of one slave, causing him to look down in puzzlement. Brona continued towards Lú's table until she stood directly opposite him, with Datho's Bowl between them. She felt terrified. Lú looked right through her, seeing only the bowl and the hall behind her.

Brona felt panic. She was not invisible to herself; what if she suddenly became visible to everyone in the hall? In her heart, she knew that Pooka wouldn't let her down. She breathed deeply and took courage once more. She must not allow the cloak to touch Lú, nor must he feel the air moving when it swept past him.

Brona stood in front of Lú for some time waiting for the right moment to lift the bowl out of his sight. Lú went on eating, drinking, talking and laughing, but never for an instant did he take his eyes off the bowl. Then the master of the feast prayed silence for the bard, and for a brief instant Lú looked across the room at him. This was Brona's moment. She threw her cloak over the bowl, and in the same movement grabbed it close to her and stepped back from the table. The bowl was certainly heavy.

She was still near the table when Lú looked back and saw that the bowl was missing. 'Where is it?' he yelled. 'Which of you has moved it? Where is the bowl I won from Maeve of the Thousand Spears?'

Everyone close to Lú began to look around them, each hoping to be the one to find the bowl. They looked under tables and benches, anywhere they thought it could be. Lú worked himself into a fury. He turned first red and then purple; he was so enraged he could scarcely speak. Each of his high nobles trembled with fear in case Lú should turn his wrath on him next.

'Where is Archeld?' Lú roared. 'It was his idea to steal the bowl. If I lose it now, people will laugh at me. Get Archeld here *now*.'

Everyone was looking at Lú; many of them were shocked that he had admitted stealing the bowl. Brona realised that, in the confusion, and with Lú continuing to rave at his court, she could get out of the hall and the palace easily. She moved as quickly as she could, being careful to avoid colliding with anyone. Outside the hall at last, and with everyone's attention still on Lú, she rested the bowl briefly on the ground to rearrange her cloak around it, before hefting it onto her shoulder. Then she hurried on, and in a few moments she had passed the guards and was out through the mighty gates of Carragdove. It was easier to carry the bowl when she could move it freely from one shoulder to the other. She set off down the hillside back to Magdawna's camp. She hoped to reach it before dawn.

When Brona was halfway back to the camp, she heard chariot wheels behind her. Had Lú's people seen her, she wondered. But how could they see an invisible person? The chariot's driver was going as fast as he could, not bothering to travel quietly. When the horse got near her, she stood well off the path, not wanting it to run her down. As it rushed by her, she thought she recognised the remains of the fiery chariot she had seen after Datho's feast, but she could not be sure. Once it had passed her, Brona returned to the path and continued her journey back to the camp.

Meanwhile, Magdawna had missed Brona and guessed what she had decided to do. He posted Dian and Finian to keep a lookout for her return. Róisín, Aidan and Rory got together quietly, away from the rest. 'Let's consult the moonstone,' Aidan suggested. 'We might be able to help Brona if she's in trouble.'

'Good idea,' Róisín agreed. 'You can look this time.'

So Aidan knelt and held up the moonstone ring for Róisín to stare at the stone, while he closed his eyes and concentrated on seeing it in his mind.

'Let other thoughts go,' Róisín said, resting her hands on

his shoulders and gazing into the jewel in his ring. 'Watch the colour fragments dancing in the moonstone's misty depths.'

Aidan lost himself in the swirl of colour until, through it, he saw shapes emerge and found himself observing Lú's great hall.

'Tell us what you see,' Róisín prompted. 'Where has the stone taken you?'

Aidan spoke slowly, as if entranced. 'Lú sits among his court,' he said. 'They are feasting. Datho's Bowl is right in front of Lú. His eyes are fixed on it.'

'Where is Brona?' Róisín asked. 'Can you see her?'

'I see only Lú and the bowl, that is all,' Aidan replied dreamily.

Róisín took her gaze away from the moonstone, wondering why, for the first time since they had begun to consult it, the stone had not revealed what they had really wanted to know. Aidan opened his eyes again.

'We'll have to wait,' Rory said, disappointed. 'I just hope Brona is all right and not in danger.'

Long before the group expected Brona back, they saw a man driving a damaged chariot with a single horse harnessed to it in the direction of their camp. 'Who are you, and what is your business at this hour?' Dian challenged him.

'I am Cruachan, Lú's master silversmith,' the man replied. 'I wish to speak with noble Rory.'

Dian had Cruachan wait while he reported to Magdawna. Magdawna and the three children all came out to speak to him. Falga, Eric and Penardun came out as well, to see what was going on.

'Greetings, Cruachan,' Rory called to him. 'Were you looking for me?'

Cruachan drew up beside them and got down from his

chariot, which was very battered-looking. 'I see with you the son of Maeve of the Thousand Spears,' he said. 'But I do not see noble Brona, queen's champion in Datho's contest.'

'What business do you have here?' Magdawna demanded, ignoring Cruachan's comment. 'Lú is no friend of ours. Why does his silversmith approach us?'

'I approach you with an offer,' Cruachan said. 'This chariot I have here is the fiery chariot that caused such trouble at the contest. I offer it to you to take back with you to Ardalba.'

'Why would we want that?' Rory asked him. 'It's a wreck.'

'It wasn't always a wreck,' Cruachan reminded him. 'It was once strong and beautiful.'

'But what use would it be to anyone now?' Rory asked.

'Think,' Cruachan said. 'If you take it back with you, perhaps Maeve's arch-druidess might discover how it shone like the sun without burning up. Then Maeve might find some other way to use this false fire.'

'What do you want for this chariot, and why would you betray Lú?' Magdawna said, doubtfully.

'I am tired of Lú and his evil ways,' Cruachan said. 'I think he should not have stolen Brona's trophy. And apart from that, he does not value my craftsmanship. He had someone else, who lives far away to the west, make this chariot and its embossed silver panels. My craftsmanship did not satisfy him. You ask what I want for bringing this to you. Since I first saw Datho's Bowl, I have wished to improve my own skill as a silversmith, until I also could produce a thing of such perfection. I want to seek out Samhain to learn from him.'

'Let him come with us,' Rory pleaded with Magdawna. 'Samhain could use some expert help and, as well as helping Cruachan improve his skills, could learn Cruachan's secret silver-working techniques.'

'That's a good idea,' Róisín said. 'We can't leave Cruachan

here alone. Someone must have missed him and the chariot by now. Who knows what Lú might do to him if he caught him?'

In the end, Magdawna agreed to let Cruachan join their party and travel with them away from Carragdove. 'We have to bring Sive back to her home first,' he warned, 'before we take you to Samhain or head south again for Ardalba.'

Everybody was so intent on talking to Cruachan that the guards had forgotten to keep their eyes on the hillside to watch for Brona coming down. When she reached the lower slopes and noticed everyone gathered around the fiery chariot and Cruachan, she knew she could pass them all easily. She went to where Magdawna's chariot was pulled up beside his weapons. Checking that no one could see her, she closed her eyes and thought of Pooka, his shining black coat and his creamy white tail and mane. 'Pooka, reveal me to mortal sight,' she breathed.

Knowing that she and Datho's Bowl were visible once more, she placed the bowl carefully on the floor of the chariot. She wound her cloak around her against the cool air. Then she went out to join the other around Lú's silversmith.

Aidan saw her first. 'Brona!' he shouted. 'You're back!'

'I knew *she* had to be the one who would take back the bowl, right from under Lú's eyes,' Cruachan cried, 'but how did I not pass her on the way down?'

They couldn't believe that she was back among them, unhurt and victorious. They hugged her and danced around her, delighted to have her with them again. She took them all to see where she had left the bowl, proof of the success of her mission. There was Samhain's masterpiece in all its beauty.

'How did you get it out of Lú's fortress?' Róisín asked.

Brona laughed. 'I walked into his judgement hall, took the bowl from right under his nose and then walked away with it,' she said, knowing none of them would believe it had been that easy.

'I was worried about you,' Rory said. 'Aidan tried to consult his moonstone to see where you were, but it couldn't find you. All it showed him was Lú feasting in his great hall.'

Brona smiled, thinking that even their moonstones were less powerful than Pooka's magic. 'Could you see the bowl in the moonstone?' she asked.

'Yes,' Rory said. 'It was on the table right in front of Lú. We wondered how you'd be able to get it out from there.'

'Well I did, didn't I?' Brona replied. 'I might have some magic of my own, mightn't I?'

Magdawna now looked with worried eyes at the first pale streaks of dawn breaking in the east. 'We must be off quickly,' he said. 'Lú will come searching for the bowl as soon as he realises that it is no longer in his fort.'

Attendants began to assemble the chariots and harness the horses. Slaves carefully wrapped the bowl in animal skins. They were all free now to help Sive find her home and family, so Aidan took bearings that would lead them north again. Once at the sea, they would follow the shoreline west until they found the lake near to which Sive's father had built his crannóg.

'Lú will expect us to travel south,' Róisín said. 'He's sure to realise that it was Maeve who sent people after him.'

'You're right,' Rory agreed. 'I wonder how far south he'll go before he realises he's chasing a will-o'-the-wisp?'

Everyone was soon ready. Aidan and Magdawna got into the leading chariot, and the rest of the party followed without a backward glance at Lú's black stronghold.

# 16

## Bringing Sive Home

By noon, the travellers could see the ocean ahead of them, dark blue and sparkling in the sunshine. Magdawna and Aidan led them right down to the shoreline along a stretch of magnificent black cliffs, which were a rusty colour in places. 'Now we know where Lú got the stone for his black palace,' Rory said. 'Look at it! You could build thousands of palaces with what's here.'

They gazed in awe at the striking rock formations. Basalt in many-sided pillars, some three times as tall as a man, stood on the edge of the land like defending soldiers. In places, the black rock formed a pavement, as if it was made of many-sided tiles. The massive scale of the scene took the children's breath away.

'That's called the Giant's Causeway,' Róisín told her three companions when the rest of the party were too far away to hear her. 'I saw pictures of it in a book. The pictures don't really give you an idea of how big it is, though.'

Rory remembered all the things Róisín had known about because she had read about them in a book. Maybe I should read more books, he thought to himself.

Eric, Falga and Penardun had never seen any cliffs like these basalt ones. 'There is nothing similar in my own country,' Eric told them, 'and not in any country where I have travelled.'

When she saw the black cliffs, Sive got very excited. 'I have never seen them before,' she told the others, 'but when I was very small, my father told me about them. He had made a special journey here as a young man. He never forgot them.'

When they had finished admiring the basalt columns, Magdawna called them together to make a start westwards. They would follow the shoreline. 'My home is on a river that flows north into a great lake connected to the sea,' Sive told them.

'Don't worry, Sive,' Magdawna assured her. 'We'll find it. Tell me if you see anything you remember along the way.'

Sive felt safe with Magdawna and the children. She knew that at last, after years of slavery, she had found friends. She became more excited each day at the thought that she was getting closer to her home.

'I wonder if my parents knew that the border folk captured me,' she said. 'They might have thought that I had drowned in our lake, or that wild animals had killed me. I am sure my father would have followed, if he had realised I had been stolen.'

'Of course he would,' Róisín assured her. 'Perhaps he *did* chase the border folk, looking for you. Soon he'll be able to tell you what happened.'

'How long were you with the border folk?' Brona asked her.

'A long time,' Sive answered. 'The winter solstice has passed three times since I was taken.'

'Are you sure they'll recognise you?' Brona asked her. 'You must have changed a lot since they last saw you.'

'It will not matter if they do not recognise me,' Sive answered with confidence. '*I* will recognise *them*.'

The whole party travelled steadily westwards, cooking their meals in the evening when the horses were tired. Cruachan nursed the fiery chariot along, trying to keep it going without breaking down. Datho's Bowl travelled in the lead chariot with Magdawna and Aidan. Eric, Falga and Penardun made the best of it in the chariots Datho had lent them, checking them for damage each evening. The spokes Falga had repaired with Rory's help were still intact.

After three days, they saw a mighty headland far in front of them, with open sea beyond. 'That must be where the shoreline turns south along the edge of the great lake Sive told us about,' Magdawna said to Aidan.

'We'll know as soon as we can see around it,' said Aidan.

Magdawna asked Sive to travel with them in the lead chariot while they drove around the base of the headland. They made an impressive procession. Magdawna and Aidan rode in the prince's chariot with Sive. Brona followed in Maeve's second racing chariot with Róisín. Then came Falga, Eric and Penardun, each one with their fighting man for protection. Cruachan went along in his damaged fiery chariot with Rory, who wanted to be with him in case the chariot needed to be repaired along the way. The others, including Dian and Finian, brought up the rear on horseback.

'You should soon begin to recognise the countryside,' Magdawna told Sive. 'Then you can guide us.'

In the afternoon, they rounded the point of the headland. They looked across a narrow channel to a headland similar to the one where they stood. 'I have been here before,' Sive told Magdawna breathlessly. 'My father took me this far in his boat so that I could see the ocean.'

Everyone was delighted to know that they had found the right lake. They turned south with the shoreline to follow this great inland waterway, knowing it would lead them to the river where Ronan had built his crannóg.

Sive's lake was enormous. At intervals along its shore were circular houses built by the fisherfolk, with some small crannógs near the water's edge. They could see no signs of dwellings further back from the water, where the open ground soon turned into woodland. There were more people living here than anywhere else the children had seen in Ardalba.

*

After two days of travelling, the lake beside them grew narrower and narrower, until they realised that it was no longer a lake but a river. Sive began to look out in earnest for her father's crannóg. 'Not much further,' she would say. 'We'll find it round the next bend.' Beyond the lake, the open ground became overgrown with trees, some of them overhanging the river bank. This made it difficult for the chariots, which now travelled more slowly, one behind the other, making their way between tall tree trunks.

'You'll know our crannóg,' Sive assured Magdawna. 'It is big, and built well out on the lake. We'll get to it by boat.'

'Sounds like Samhain's,' Aidan said. 'Your father must be an important man.'

'He is,' Sive said. 'He is a master craftsman. No one in all the land can make a better chariot.'

The evening sun was hanging on golden clouds near the western horizon when they rounded yet another turn in this winding river and came to a small, sandy beach. In front of them, far out on the river, beyond sedges and reeds, was an impressive crannóg. A strong fence of sharply pointed stakes enclosed three small circular wattle dwellings, as well as a cooking area and an animal enclosure, where hens and piglets ran around. Dominating all this stood the master's dwelling, a large wooden building with a sturdy thatched roof.

Sive could hardly speak. 'That's it,' she whispered. 'That's my home. I thought I would never see it again.'

# 17

## SIVE FINDS HER FAMILY

The whole party came to a halt opposite the crannóg. Sive could not take her eyes off the building. She had pictured it so often, thinking she would never see it again. Tears of happiness ran down her cheeks, and she wiped them away with her hand. Róisín left her chariot and came over to Sive. 'Not long now,' she said. 'Soon you will be with your family and you'll never feel lonely again.'

Meanwhile, Magdawna had asked among his slaves and soldiers to find out if anyone had brought along a bodhrán. No one had, but one of Datho's fighting men had a small horn with him. 'Try it,' Magdawna said. 'It may be loud enough for those at the crannóg to hear us.'

The fighting man stood on the river bank and held his horn high before him, blowing into it as hard as he could. The sound it made was sweetly mournful. 'Try again,' Magdawna said, when he saw no movement at the settlement. 'Keep trying for a while. Sometimes sound carries well over water.'

The fighting man stood on the beach and blew his horn at short intervals. Before long, he saw movement at the crannóg, and called Magdawna. They both watched closely until they saw that slaves were getting a boat ready to cross over to them. Soon, faintly across the water, they heard men singing rhythmically to the dip of oars, their singing increasing in volume the closer they got to the shore.

When the craft was halfway across, the watchers could easily see those who travelled in it. The central figure was a mighty, broad-shouldered man. Strands of his untidy brown hair blew around him in the breeze caused by the movement of the boat, making his large head seem even bigger under its helmet of polished leather. In his huge hands he held his sword by its hilt, its tip pointing down between his knees to rest on the hull of the leather boat. Many silver bands circled his sinewy arms, and a large silver pin held his woven purple cloak at his shoulder. His face was grave and commanding. Behind him, a young man held his master's spear and his leather shield. Sive could not take her eyes off this imposing man. 'My father,' she whispered to Róisín. 'After all this time, I've found him.'

Still several oars' length from land, the master halted the boat and hailed Magdawna. 'Who summons Ronan from his crannóg, and for what purpose?' he demanded.

'Master craftsman,' Magdawna replied, 'we come in the first place from Maeve of the Thousand Spears, wife of Ailill, King of the West, whose son and champion I am. We are now on our way from Lú's stronghold at Carragdove far in the north. We are travelling back to the kingdom of Ardalba.'

The man held up his hand to stop Magdawna. 'My crannóg is not on your route from Carragdove in the north to Ardalba in the west,' he said. 'What brings you here?'

'We have come out of our way to reach you,' Magdawna said. 'In the north, far from here, we met a girl held in slavery who asked us for help in finding her way home.' Ardalba's prince turned to Sive, holding out his hand to her. She took it and stepped forward right to the water's edge. 'I am Sive,' she said in firm tones, 'daughter of Ronan the chariot-maker. Do you not recognise me, Father?'

Ronan stared at Sive. He stood up in the boat so that he could see her better. Then with a shout he leaped into the shallow water and rushed across to take her in his arms. 'Sive! My Sive!' he exclaimed. 'We looked everywhere for you. We thought you were dead.' They stood then in a silent embrace until Ronan at last pulled back. 'I am forgetting my manners,' he said to Magdawna. 'My joy at recovering my daughter has made me forget my debt to those who have restored her to me.'

Ronan arranged with Magdawna to leave some of his own crannóg slaves with Magdawna's to guard their chariots for the night. 'You must all come with me,' Ronan said to the travellers. 'We will have feasting and celebration until day dawns. And we will not forget to send a share to those who guard your horses and chariots.'

He looked across and noticed Cruachan and the fiery chariot. 'That is my handiwork,' he said, pointing to the chariot. 'Who has reduced it to this pathetic state?'

'Was it you who made this for Lú?' Cruachan asked. 'I knew only that he rejected my work and sought better. It was Lú and his anti-druid Archeld who damaged your masterpiece.'

'I see clever repair work,' Ronan said. 'Who did that?'

'Some I did myself,' Cruachan answered, 'but I could not have done it all or finished it so well without the expert help of noble Rory.'

Ronan glanced at Rory, who blushed deeply. 'I see a man with gifted hands, a craftsman in the making,' Ronan said. 'I could do with an apprentice like you.'

Rory looked at his hands in confusion. They looked ordinary to him. 'Was it you who fixed the fiery chariot to shine so brightly that it almost blinded people?' he asked Ronan, to change the subject.

'No,' Ronan replied. 'I made a decorated racing chariot, no more. Lú asked me to embed small pieces of rose quartz in the wooden side-panels, where they would be hidden under the embossed-silver sheeting. I thought nothing of this, considering them to be no more than good-luck charms.'

'It must have been Archeld,' Cruachan muttered. 'He probably needed those quartz pieces to help him work his mischief.'

Magdawna was pleased to have Ronan's extra guards for the night, to protect Datho's three chariots as well as his own, and to keep Datho's Bowl safe until morning. 'Cruachan will come with us to your crannóg,' Magdawna said to Ronan, 'and if your storyteller permits, we will let you know everything that has brought us here when you are ready to hear it after the feasting and mead-drinking. No epic saga could entertain you more.'

Ronan laughed. 'We'll wait, so,' he said, turning to get into his boat again, 'but your tale had better be good.'

Sive went back in the boat with her father. It returned three times to collect the four children, the three charioteers, and Magdawna and Cruachan, and bring them all to Ronan's great crannóg. When the children arrived, Sive brought them inside to greet her mother, Alva, who hugged each of them in turn. 'How can I thank you?' she asked. 'We thought Sive was dead. We can scarcely believe our happiness.'

Attendants took Sive away to dress and ornament her as was fitting for the daughter of the house. Róisín and Brona went with her, while Aidan and Rory stayed with Magdawna and the charioteers. Cooks prepared one of Ronan's best pigs and placed it on a spit. Alva supervised everything, making sure there would be plenty of food and mead.

When the sun had gone down, the banquet began. Róisín and Brona, and Sive's own attendants, brought her in to be presented to the whole household. Ronan stood to receive her. 'This is my daughter whom we thought was dead – Sive, daughter of Ronan and Alva,' he declared proudly.

Everybody clapped and cheered and stamped their feet, while Sive stood between her mother and father, holding their hands. Attendants had brushed and braided her long brown hair until it shone. They had arranged it in thin plaits, which they tied up by their ends to make graceful loops around her head and neck. Into the plaits they wove gold and amethyst beads that glittered in the light cast by many tapers. Sive wore a fine linen gown the colour of amethyst, held with gold clasps at her shoulders and bound at her waist with a gold belt. A green cloak matched her green eyes; it was made of fine woollen fabric and was heavily embroidered with gold thread. Her slippers were of doeskin, and were soft and warm. Róisín and Brona also wore beautiful clothes for the celebrations, but Sive was truly the most beautiful girl at the feast that night. 'These are the clothes my mother wore at her wedding,' Sive told the others afterwards, her green eyes shining. 'My father was so proud of her.'

Aidan and Rory entered the crannóg as the feast was about to begin. They once again wore the garments of high nobles: soft white tunics and amethyst cloaks. Ronan's guards and members of his household wore clothes the colour of purple heather.

The master of the feast soon signalled for food to be brought in, and everyone began to enjoy themselves. Ronan and Alva sat on either side of Sive to make sure that she wanted for nothing. Magdawna and the four children enjoyed other positions of honour, as did Falga, Eric and Penardun. Cruachan, himself a master craftsman, was placed close to Ronan. The craftsman could not take his eyes off Sive, who looked radiant with happiness. Slaves poured mead from jugs until the jewelled drinking vessels flowed over. After living simply for so long on their journeys, the travellers from Ardalba appreciated Ronan's lavish hospitality. It was good to eat and drink at their ease, instead of camping in the open, with the constant threat of attack.

After everyone had satisfied their hunger, the music and entertainment began. Ronan's harper excelled himself, singing in praise of Sive and her rescuers until they were all deeply embarrassed. 'Stop him, Father,' Sive begged, laughing. 'It's too much. It was all much more ordinary than that.'

The harper laughed too, and began another verse with even more exaggerated descriptions of everyone's bravery. Ronan smiled, but at the end of the verse he interrupted to suggest that it might be time for storytelling. 'If my storyteller does not object,' he said, 'we would call on our visitors to tell their own story.'

Everyone clapped and stamped their feet, and Ronan's storyteller offered his seat to the visitors. They looked at each other. Who was to do the telling? 'Let Maeve's high nobles tell their own tale,' Magdawna said, 'and I will finish with an account of how we found Ronan's crannóg for Sive.'

This pleased the company. The children conferred for a moment. They decided that Róisín should start the story. She took her place on the storyteller's seat and began her tale with the arrival of Datho's messenger to challenge Maeve to race for Datho's Bowl. The listeners heard of all their adventures since then. Brona did not mention Pooka or the fact that he had given her the gift of invisibility. Magdawna finished the tale by describing their journey to the basalt cliffs of the north, from there along the coast to the great lake, and finally to Ronan's crannóg on the river. When he came to the end, a sigh of satisfaction rose from the listeners.

'Never have we heard such a tale,' Ronan said. He gave

orders for more tapers to be lit, and for fuel to be added to the fire. Then he had attendants fill every cup before he began to speak. 'I wish to salute Maeve's high nobles,' he said, his embossed-silver goblet in his right hand. All the guests fell silent. 'I salute Róisín for the comfort and encouragement she has given to Sive since first they met,' he said. 'I salute Brona, queen's champion, and winner of Datho's great race. I salute Rory for his expertise in chariot repair, and for the assistance he has given Cruachan in repairing what is now known as the fiery chariot. And I salute Aidan for his mystic understanding of the movement of heavenly bodies, which enables him to find his way throughout the land. Let us drink to these high nobles.'

All those at the feast stood to drink to the four children. Aidan, Róisín, Brona and Rory did not know where to look, they were so embarrassed by all this praise. When the cheering had stopped, Rory stood up to thank Ronan and all who had joined in his toast. 'We don't deserve this praise,' he said. 'We are high nobles of Maeve of the Thousand Spears. It was our duty to serve her, and Ardalba.'

When the feast was over, Ronan promised that in the morning he would take the children to see some of the chariots he had made. 'I am good at making them,' he told them modestly. 'There are no better chariots than mine in all the land.'

Magdawna, not to be outdone, promised to show Datho's Bowl to Ronan. 'You will never see its like again,' he said. 'There is no other bowl so perfect in all the land.'

Slaves had spread bearskins around the crannóg's walls. Everyone found a place to sleep, their feet warmed by the fire, which was still smouldering in its brazier. The children felt secure for the night in this safe lake-dwelling.

# 18

## RONAN'S CHARIOTS

Morning dawned misty over Ronan's crannóg. The river bank seemed remote, almost invisible. After a breakfast of oatmeal sweetened with honey, Ronan took the visitors to his workshop to see his finished chariots. By then, the haze was lifting from the river and the strengthening sun was turning the surrounding landscape a vivid green. 'Let's stop at my camp on the way,' Magdawna suggested. 'We can show you Datho's Bowl. Then my guards can wrap it up securely for our long journey home.'

Ronan's boat had to make three journeys from the crannóg in order to bring to land everyone who wanted to come. This included Sive, who Ronan insisted should still wear her magnificent clothes as daughter of the house. She could not yet bear to let her father out of her sight, even for a moment, and followed wherever he went. Róisín and Brona stayed with her as much as they could that day, knowing that soon they would have to leave her and return to Ardalba.

Once they were on shore, it was a short walk to Magdawna's camp. Ronan was made welcome there. Dian and Finian unwrapped the bowl and placed it carefully on the ground before him. It was some time since the children had had a good look at this work of art. Now they were as speechless as Ronan. The wide triangular shape of the bowl was perfect. Its thick silver shone without a scratch or blemish, reflecting the sunlight so brightly that people might think the dazzling radiance came from within the metal itself. There was no design of any kind on the bowl; its beauty was in its shape and proportion, qualities of craftsmanship that no person present had ever seen equalled. The children had seen other examples of Samhain's work, but none of them had been as perfect as this dazzling object.

'Thank you for letting me see this masterpiece,' Ronan said to Magdawna. 'It can have no equal, not only throughout this land, but in any land.'

Falga, Eric and Penardun had never viewed the bowl properly before. They agreed now with Ronan that they had never seen its like, not on Man, not in the Land of Dragons, and not in the Northern Lands where Eric had been born.

When all had looked long enough at Datho's Bowl to be sure they would never forget it, no matter how long they lived, Magdawna gave orders for it to be wrapped securely and packed for its journey back to Ardalba. 'Now,' he said to Ronan, 'we are impatient to see your chariots. I heard that no one can surpass your skill in making them.'

Ronan gave a proud smile. 'That is true,' he said. 'I have yet to meet the man who can make a better chariot than me. Come! I will show you.' He led them from the river to where a wall of rock rose in front of them. In this wall was the entrance, which was shielded from view by thick bushes and guarded by slaves. 'I could not leave this place un-guarded,' Ronan said to Magdawna, 'not with such riches inside.' He led them into a wide, high-ceilinged chamber. They expected it to be dark inside, but each corner was bathed in mellow light. Ronan pointed upward: the ceiling spiralled towards the roof, and they saw openings at each corner, through which shafts of sunlight shone, dancing with dust particles. Along one side of the chamber stood Ronan's workbench. On its right his tools were carefully laid out, and on its left stood some unfinished wheels and half-worked pieces.

'Come,' he said, 'let me show you my treasures.' He led them to the back of the workspace to a spot where wood was stacked. Ronan moved half a dozen logs to reveal the entrance to an inner chamber, which he invited them to enter. One by one they stepped through into a cathedral-like area, now lit by torches set into sconces along one wall. In this flickering light stood five magnificent chariots, finished, polished and ready to be used.

'I am well known for working quickly, for finishing a chariot in record time,' said Ronan, with a laugh. 'Here you see my secret. I always keep finished chariots here. Then, when I get an order from some king or minor lord, the most I have to do is to make small changes to the design, or alter the decoration. They think I possess magical power from the Otherworld to produce a chariot so quickly.'

They were delighted to have the chance to look around and admire Ronan's work. Cruachan was particularly interested in seeing how these chariots were made, and in inspecting their lovely inlays, the silverwork on their wheels and their ornamental side panels. Brona was interested in looking at the bronze horse bits Ronan had designed for the horses that would pull the chariots. The horse bits looked much better than any she had seen in Ardalba. She thought she could persuade Maeve to consider using this improved design.

Magdawna saw at once how superior Ronan's chariots were to the two the children had brought from Ardalba – his own champion's chariot and Maeve's racing chariot, both of which had raced in Datho's race. 'It is a pity you dwell so far from us, master craftsman,' Magdawna said. 'My mother and I could have done business with you.'

'A pity indeed, prince,' Ronan replied.

All this time, Ronan had been watching Cruachan and Rory. They had examined every part of every chariot to see exactly how they had been put together. Meanwhile, Róisín and Sive climbed into a chariot each and imagined that they were holding the reins of the world's most beautiful horses.

Aidan also examined the chariots and acknowledged Ronan's excellent work. Privately, he thought chariots were cumbersome in a land where there were no roads. It was hard to get a chariot over rough ground or through woodland, as he knew from experience. But he had to agree that the chariots were beautiful.

The sun was beginning to go down again. Ronan thought it was time to return to the crannóg. They got ready to go back to the spot where they had left the boat. Magdawna decided to walk back with Ronan. 'We'll have to leave you tomorrow morning,' he said. 'We've been away from home for too long. My mother will become anxious about us.'

'So soon?' Ronan asked in surprise. 'I need to think of how to repay you for your kindness in bringing my daughter home.'

'You owe me nothing,' Magdawna replied. 'Sive saved the four children, who are precious to Maeve, from attack by the border folk, who had held her in slavery. Later, she fought like a warrior when robbers attacked us. Did you know that she is deadly with a slingshot?' Magdawna smiled when he thought of this. 'We were glad to help her find you.'

'Nevertheless,' Ronan insisted, 'I am bound in honour to repay good done to me, and for Sive no price is too great.' He thought for a few moments. Then a smile slowly crossed his face. 'You have admired my chariots. Take three of them, and I shall have two left to trade.'

'I cannot take payment for helping Sive,' Magdawna replied, 'but I see a way that might satisfy both of us.'

'And what is that?'

'Falga, Penardun and Eric travelled with the children to protect them when they followed Lú of the North to recapture Datho's Bowl. Their own chariots were destroyed during the race by Lú's anti-druid, Archeld, and they are driving chariots lent by Datho. Would you consider giving each of *them* one of your chariots?'

Ronan was delighted with this suggestion. There and then, he told everyone to return to the cave. He let the three men choose a chariot each, and two horses apiece to complete the gift. They could scarcely believe Ronan's generosity, and thanked him repeatedly. 'You have saved me a long, long walk back to the Northern Lands,' Eric said, smiling.

Returning to the crannóg, Falga, Eric and Penardun brought their new chariots back to Magdawna's camp. They left Dian and Finian guarding them, before going on to Ronan's dwelling. The feasting was quite a sad event, as everyone knew that in the morning Magdawna's party would depart for home.

When the mead was flowing after the feast, Ronan formally thanked his visitors again for helping his daughter to return to her home. Falga, speaking for the three charioteers, thanked Ronan for his magnificent gift to them. Róisín spoke for the children, saying how much they had enjoyed their short stay with Ronan and how lonely they would be to leave Sive. Magdawna finished by telling Ronan how grateful his mother, Maeve of the Thousand Spears, would be when she heard of Ronan's kind reception of them.

Next morning dawned bright and clear. When they had

eaten, Ronan got them all across the river and back to Magdawna's camp to make the final preparations for their journey. Sive and her mother, Alva, came with them.

Falga, Eric and Penardun were the first to go. They would travel south-east together for a time. Then Falga would head directly east, to seek a boat sailing for Man. Eric and Penardun would go further south before crossing the sea to take them to the Land of Dragons. From Penardun's home there, Eric would continue on and cross more seas before reaching his home in the distant Northern Lands.

Before getting into their new chariots, the three men said sad goodbyes to everybody. The children gave each of them a hug. 'Goodbye,' they said. 'Safe journey.' The charioteers hugged them back. 'It was a great adventure,' the men said. 'We're glad Brona got the bowl back. And we're glad that Sive found her home.' Magdawna arm-clasped each of them in farewell. Then they got into their chariots and drove away.

'Goodbye,' the others called after them. The four children sang Samhain's song as loudly as they could.

Then it was Magdawna's turn to lead his people away. The children said goodbye to Ronan, who arm-clasped them warmly. 'Remember,' he said to Rory, 'you will always be welcome as my apprentice.'

The four then said goodbye to Sive. Róisín and Brona threw their arms around her. 'We'll miss you,' they said. 'But we're glad you're home again.' Aidan and Rory said their sad goodbyes too. They would never forget how she had laid low the robbers from her perch in the trees over their heads. Last of all, Ronan bade goodbye to Cruachan. 'Change your mind. Stay and work with me,' Ronan urged. 'I will make chariots, and you can do all the metalwork and decoration. We will become famous together.'

'I have a dream,' Cruachan said, shaking his head. 'Before I die, I want to make a bowl as perfect as Datho's Bowl. Only Samhain can teach me to do that.'

'But will he show another silversmith his secrets?' Ronan asked. 'If you change your mind about working with him, turn around and come straight back to me. Together we can make masterpieces.'

Cruachan took his arm with tears in his eyes. 'You are a good man, Ronan. I will think about what you say.'

Sive came over to Cruachan then. She, too, had tears in her eyes and could scarcely speak. 'Goodbye,' she said in a small voice. 'I will miss you more than anyone else. Perhaps you *will* return to my father some day.' Cruachan looked at her in amazement. In all his life, Cruachan had never had anybody who cared about him. And now to think that this beautiful girl would miss him!

Magdawna set off with Aidan in his chariot, and one by one each chariot rolled after his. Ronan's people stood to watch them depart. His harper played a cheerful march to set them on their way. When they could hear it no longer, they knew they had left Sive and Ronan behind them at last.

# 19

## Datho's Bowl Goes Home

Magdawna led his party south. Aidan took his usual sightings of the sun by day and the pole star by night. 'How can you tell the direction like that?' Magdawna asked him.

Aidan laughed and said, 'Your mother thinks we have special powers. This is one of mine.'

When the others were out of earshot, he told Brona, Rory and Róisín where he was heading. 'Think of the map of Ireland,' he said. 'If we go in a straight line from where we are, we should come to the Erne where it flows between its two lakes. We should be able to cross it there.'

'You are a great navigator,' Róisín said. '*I* couldn't wander around this wild country with only the stars to guide me.'

'You could if you had done as much orienteering as I have,' Aidan said. 'The difference here is that I use the sun instead of a compass. When great explorers went to new places, they didn't have roads or signposts. How do you think *they* managed? In early times, they didn't even have compasses.'

'How did Magdawna find *his* way when he followed us north?' Rory wondered. 'He's relying on you now, and he admits he can't use stars.'

'We were a large party of five chariots and several horses with riders. We left clear tracks, which Magdawna could follow, and he could ask people he met if they had seen us, and how far ahead of him they thought we were.'

The travellers had been away from Ardalba for a long time, and all they wanted now was to get safely back there. Each day they moved steadily along. Every evening their attendants prepared food. Sometimes it was fish caught in lakes or streams; other times it was meat from small animals hunted by Datho's fighting men. Each night they slept wrapped in their cloaks under starlit skies.

One day, from a small hill Aidan saw distant water ahead. 'We're nearly there,' he shouted to the others. 'We can cross the river that flows out of that lake.'

Magdawna suggested that they continue to the lake before evening, and then move downriver until they came to a ford. When they had reached the ford, they ate their evening meal and camped for the night.

Next morning they got ready to cross the river, to begin the last leg of their journey. Chariots stood in line to traverse the ford first, with riders and their horses waiting behind them. Suddenly Cruachan in the fiery chariot shouted out to Magdawna in the lead: 'Wait! I've changed my mind. I can't go with you. I'm going back to Ronan!'

Magdawna was surprised. 'I thought you had a dream!' he shouted back. 'I thought you wanted to study silverwork with Samhain. You have to be sure that this is what you really want. Once we leave you, you will be on your own.'

'I know that,' Cruachan said, 'but this *is* what I really want. I've thought of nothing else since leaving the crannóg. I have to be honest with myself: I could never match Samhain's skill in silver-craft, no matter how he tried to help me. But working with Ronan and learning from him, I think I *could* excel at making chariots.'

'Ronan did invite you to join him,' Róisín said doubtfully.

'It's just that you seemed so determined to reach Samhain.'

'Ronan is a good man,' Cruachan said. 'I know I could work well with him.' He paused. 'And then there's Sive.'

Róisín's eyebrows shot up, her dark blue eyes opening wide. 'Sive! What has Sive got to do with it?'

Cruachan looked at his feet. 'I miss her,' he said forlornly. 'I miss her more with each day's travel I put between us. I can't leave her.'

Magdawna laughed. 'Now all is clear,' he said. 'Now I know you really have thought everything through. But are you sure that Ronan, who invited you only to work with him, will be willing to give you his daughter?'

Cruachan smiled for the first time. 'I think he might,' he said. 'I would not really be taking her from him at all. He would see her every day.'

The children got up to hug Cruachan and thump him on the back, they were so delighted for him. They knew he would be happy with Sive, and they had all seen how sad she had been when she said goodbye to him.

Magdawna appointed Rory as the new driver of the fiery chariot and gave Cruachan the horse he had taken from Lú when he drove the fiery chariot away from Carragdove. Cruachan could ride that on his return journey to Ronan's crannóg. 'We owe you that,' Magdawna said. 'It's the least we can do for you in return for your gift of the fiery chariot. Who knows what Maeve and Scathach will learn from that?'

'You'll have no trouble finding your way back if you follow our tracks,' Aidan reassured him.

'I'll have no one to help me if we break another spoke on the way home,' Rory said sadly. 'Goodbye, Cruachan. I'll miss you.'

Brona and Róisín both hugged him. 'Take care of Sive,' they said. 'She is as brave as you are, but she had a hard time as a slave. It is her turn to be happy.'

By now, Cruachan was smiling so hard it hurt his face. He could scarcely believe how much he obviously meant to the four children. He hardly dared hope that at last he would have a real home to go to, with Ronan's household and Sive.

Magdawna had Cruachan's horse brought up, and made sure he had what he would need for travelling alone. He gave his friend a warm hand-clasp. 'Go safely,' he said. 'My mother will be thankful to you for the fiery chariot.'

Cruachan mounted his horse, waving goodbye to the fighting men, guards and slaves whom he had come to know so well. He counted each one as a friend. Then he turned round and shouted back to the children: 'Tell Samhain why I changed my mind. Tell him I wish him well always.' Finally he turned his horse's head back towards north and walked it quietly away.

The children felt sad that they might never see Cruachan again, but one thing they had learned in Ardalba's world was that you never knew what the future might hold. After their first adventure there, they had not expected to meet Cruachan again, or to become friends with him, as they had done now.

As soon as Cruachan had ridden out of sight, Magdawna lined up the chariots once more, with the rest of the party behind them. He led them across the ford, and from there they continued their journey south.

\*

After several more days of travel, they saw mountains ahead. Aidan decided it would be easier to go around them than to try to go over them. They followed a large semicircle to keep the mountains on their left. When they had gone all the way around them, Aidan could see another large lake in front and to the right of them, and he guided the chariots in that direction to camp for the night.

The four children went for a walk after they had eaten, to loosen up after a day of bumping along in their chariots. 'That lake where we're camping has to be Lough Allen,' Aidan said. 'All we have to do now is follow Shining River until it reaches Wild Deer Lake. Then we follow the lakeside south until we come to Samhain's crannóg. We'll be almost in Ardalba then.'

This was great news. Everyone was tired of travelling – tired of driving chariots, of sleeping in the open, of eating whatever food they could find on their way. They looked forward to perfumed baths heated by slaves, to attendants to dress their hair and help them with their high nobles' banquet clothes, to sleeping in their own luxurious rooms in Maeve's white palace. 'A few more days and we'll be there,' Aidan said, encouraging them.

'In a way, I'll miss all this,' Rory said. 'It was exciting all the time.'

'Yes, but I could do with a bit less excitement now,' Róisín said. 'I'd like to be warm and clean, and to sleep in a proper bed.'

'The person I most want to see is Scathach,' Brona told them. 'I want to learn more from her while I can.'

Next morning they all set off again, following the river, as Aidan had suggested. 'How can you tell that this will bring us to Samhain's lake?' Magdawna asked him. 'We have passed many rivers and small lakes since we left Ronan's house. What's special about this one?'

'I'm good at finding my way,' Aidan said. 'I've spent a lot of time learning how to do it.'

'You mean someone taught you how to do it?' a crafty

look spread over Magdawna's face. 'Then when we're back in my mother's palace, you'll be able to teach me?'

'I'm not sure you could learn,' Aidan said. 'You don't have a picture of the whole land in your head, as I have. Other skills are called for too, which do not exist in this era. You forget that I am from a distant place and a far future time.' Magdawna said no more, but Aidan knew he would not forget about it.

The weather changed. Rain sheeted down over them for hours. They sheltered where they could, but everybody got wet. After a couple of days, Shining River burst its banks and the land was flooded. In low cloud, and with the flood waters spreading, Aidan found it difficult to keep to his path. He feared they would miss the crannóg.

But he had forgotten the fisherfolk. Before Magdawna's party could glimpse the crannóg, the fisherfolk had caught sight of them. Their leader, bringing some of his people with him, came to meet this important group of nobles riding in chariots. While he bowed and greeted Magdawna in the lead chariot, Róisín saw Merle standing behind him. 'Merle!' she called. 'It's us. Don't you remember?'

The fisherfolk looked at Róisín, suddenly recognising the girl who had nursed Samhain after a wild boar had almost killed him. Then they saw Aidan, Rory and Brona in the other chariots, and remembered the part they had played in Samhain's rescue. 'Welcome! Welcome!' they cried, coming up to each of the children in turn to greet them.

It was several minutes before Róisín could introduce Magdawna, whom they had never seen before. 'This is Magdawna, Prince of Ardalba,' she said formally, 'son of Maeve of the Thousand Spears, and of Ailill, High Lord of the West.'

The fisherfolk and their leader bowed low before Magdawna, who returned their greeting with dignity. Then Merle stood in the leading chariot with Magdawna, to guide them all to Samhain's crannóg. They would not have found it easily. Because of the heavy rain and the river breaking its banks, the crannóg seemed much further from land than they remembered it. The small beach where the coracle had come from was now under water. Merle directed them to a spot further along.

Datho's fighting man had to blow his horn again, as he had done at Ronan's crannóg, to summon the boat to come for them. He had to blow for a long time. Someone out on the lake heard them at last, and they saw the coracle setting out towards them.

The children were dying to meet Samhain again. As soon as they heard people on the boat singing the rowers' song, they joined in as loudly as they could. When the coracle drew near, they could see it was Samhain himself who had come to collect them. Soon he was thumping them on the back and shaking their arms, laughing with delight to see them. He also welcomed Magdawna, whom he had met during Datho's race.

Before long, Magdawna had left the fisherfolk in charge of his chariots, and the coracle made several trips to bring everyone to Samhain's dwelling for a feast. Cormac, Samhain's son, was there to greet them; he couldn't wait to hear all their news. After a magnificent meal and plenty of mead, everyone settled down to hear about their quest, and how Brona had got back Datho's Bowl. That was when they told Samhain about Cruachan, and passed on his good wishes.

Samhain laughed out loud. 'Cruachan made the right decision,' he said. 'He is good but could never show skill equal to mine. And didn't he steal my bowl in the first place? Without Rory, we would never have seen it again.'

Next morning, after fond farewells at the crannóg, Samhain had the coracle bring them back to where they had left their chariots. It was there that Magdawna told the children that he would not go back with them to Ardalba. 'You are at the borders of my mother's kingdom now,' he told them, 'and you know your way to Ardalba. It is *your* privilege to return Datho's Bowl to my mother. I will take Datho's chariots, horses, fighting men and slaves safely back to him. Then I will follow you. I will not be far behind you. I will ride my own horse back, the one I rode north to catch up with you. That will get me home faster than any chariot.'

The children were sorry that the prince would not continue with them, but they knew how helpful Datho had been when they had first set out in pursuit of Lú. It was only right to return his people and his property safely and with due thanks.

'Goodbye,' Magdawna called back to them from his chariot. 'I'll only be a day or two behind you.' Then he urged his horses forward and was soon out of sight.

The four looked at each other and smiled, glad to be on their own once again.

## 20

## MAEVE RECEIVES HER TROPHY

When Magdawna had gone, the children discussed how they would continue their journey. Brona and Róisín would lead in Magdawna's racing chariot, and Aidan and Dian would follow in Maeve's second chariot. Rory would drive the fiery chariot, and Finian would ride with him.

'That's settled, then,' Rory said. 'We'd better get started.'

'We head straight out from the lake, don't we?' asked Brona.

'That's right,' Aidan said. 'We'll have to go carefully through any woodland so as not to damage our chariots, but soon we should see Sleeping Dog Mountain.'

They set off then, making good time where the ground was flat, and slowing down wherever they met trees. By noon, they could see, far away on their left, signs of the forest fire they had battled through on their way to Wild Deer Lake.

'That fire was just coincidence,' Róisín said to Brona. 'I don't think Lú had anything to do with it. His magic chariot was the real threat all along.'

'You could be right,' Brona agreed, 'but I don't believe in coincidence. I think Archeld was making doubly sure that his master would win the race.'

Later in the day, as they were emerging from a forest,

they saw Sleeping Dog Mountain far in front of them. 'Do you think we'll get to Ardalba before nightfall?' Rory asked Aidan when they stopped to rest the horses.

'We will need to take the horses and chariots carefully over that mountain,' Aidan said. 'We should do it before darkness falls. What do you think?'

'I think we should cross quickly over the mountain, camp there, then ride into Ardalba fort in late morning,' Rory said. 'Our return with the trophy is a great victory for Maeve. Brona should carry Datho's Bowl into the fort – if it's not too heavy for her – so that everyone can see it. It will be a state occasion.'

When they reached the base of Sleeping Dog Mountain, Róisín, Dian and Finian got down to lead the horses up the incline, glad that the slope was gentle and the surface not rocky. Soon they reached the summit and continued down the other side, coming to the foot of the mountain before it grew dark. They stopped here to make camp for the last time.

After their meal, they talked about the best way to make a dramatic return to Ardalba. Brona and Róisín agreed with Aidan and Rory that it would be an important moment for the queen. 'And Brona deserves a victory march too,' Róisín said. 'She won the bowl, and then she got it back from Lú all by herself, didn't she.'

Brona blushed. She alone knew that she had not got the bowl back all by herself. She would have liked to tell everyone about Pooka's part in it, but she could not break her promise to him. 'Our return *will* be ceremonial,' she said. 'I should carry the trophy high over my head for all to see while you drive the chariot, Róisín.'

'You'll never hold that over your head,' Rory said, remembering his own problems in carrying it.

Brona stared at him with her dark brown eyes. 'I carried it out of Lú's stronghold,' she reminded him, 'and I brought it down the hill to our camp. I have special powers, haven't I.'

The other three looked at Brona proudly. 'If you think you can do it,' Rory said, 'then you can. It doesn't always take magic.' They then wrapped their cloaks around them and slept soundly under the stars.

Next morning bright sunshine shone through the fine fog. They saw green countryside stretching out before them. The children prepared themselves for their entry to Ardalba. Discarding their travelling clothes, Brona and Aidan put on the tunics and white cloaks they had worn in Datho's race. Róisín and Rory dressed as they had for Datho's feast. Dian and Finian polished their spears and shields until they shone and shook the dust out of their white cloaks. 'No one will look at us,' they told the children, laughing. '*We* are not high nobles.'

'Do you want to practise holding up the bowl?' Róisín asked Brona.

Brona shook her head. She knew she could not lift the bowl without help from Pooka. She would not look for his help until the time came.

The party set off for Ardalba. As the mountain behind them grew smaller, ahead of them Maeve's white palace became clearer. They did not hurry, but walked the horses in the order they had decided on for their entry to the fort. Long before they got there, Maeve's lookouts saw them approaching and alerted everyone in the stronghold that they were on their way. Slaves and nobles alike spilled out to greet the children, who had worked so well for Ardalba's ruler. They lined up on each side of the path, waiting to form a guard of honour.

'We'll have to stop and get ourselves into proper order

for a procession,' Brona said. 'Before we reach the waiting rows of nobles and attendants, I'll lift up Datho's Bowl so that everyone can see it.'

'You'll never do it,' Rory warned. 'Even if you *could* lift it over your head, you could never keep it there all the way to the palace.'

'I can if I *think* I can,' Brona said quickly. 'You told me so yourself.'

They got the chariots in line and set off at a fast walk towards the waiting crowd. When they still had a little way to go, Brona called a halt. While Róisín unwrapped the bowl from its protective covers, Brona stood with her eyes closed, gathering her mental power before calling secretly on Pooka. *Pooka!* she whispered in her mind. *Pooka, I must lift the bowl before all the people. You made me strong to win it, my horses strong to race for it. Lend me your strength now, to raise it up and keep it raised.*

Brona felt no different. She told Róisín it was time to get the chariot moving again towards the fort. Róisín kept the horses at a steady walk. When they had come almost as far as the line of waiting people, Brona bent to pick up the bowl. It was as heavy as lead. Then, pulling it upwards until she stood straight in the chariot, Brona saw Pooka ahead of her. It was as if he was running backwards, keeping his head towards her.

He was close enough to her now to blow fire from his nostrils into her face. Brona breathed in this fire, and suddenly she felt strong and free and happy. The bowl seemed to weigh nothing. Laughing in victory, she raised it above her head, and to Rory's amazement, kept it there for the rest of the journey. Only Brona could see the Wild Horse of the Mountain who shared his power with her, shaking his white mane while he breathed strength towards her.

Maeve's high nobles and her whole household cheered and clapped and stamped their feet when they saw the trophy. It was proof that Ardalba was the greatest kingdom in the land. And it was double proof that Maeve was mightier than Lú: he had not won the race in the first place, nor had he been able to keep the trophy after he had stolen it from her.

The procession passed through lines of watchers, who fell in behind Rory's chariot to follow the children on foot, until there was a long line of people moving towards the fort. When the children drew close to the fort, Róisín saw Maeve standing with Ailill at the entrance. Beside her stood Scathach, a large wolfhound seated on each side of her, the dogs' huge heads resting on their paws.

The nearer they came to the royal party, the noisier the crowd became. When they stood in front of Maeve and Ailill, Róisín brought the chariot gently to a halt. At that moment, the crowd fell silent. Brona stepped down carefully onto the ground, still holding the bowl on high. She saw Pooka walking beside her now. On she went, until she stood directly in front of Maeve of the Thousand Spears, whose violet eyes were glowing with pride.

Slowly Brona lowered the massive silver trophy and placed it on the ground at Maeve's feet. When she had done that, she saw Pooka gallop into the sky and disappear from view. She knew she could not have held the bowl aloft for another second.

## 21

## The Secret of the Fiery Chariot

Brona stood before Maeve and bowed deeply. The queen was almost too moved to speak. She rested her hand on Brona's head. 'My true champion,' she said. 'I now decree that you will always carry that title, even when your time as champion has passed. You are all my champions,' she continued, looking at the other children. 'Noble Brona could not have accomplished alone all that she has achieved with your help and support.'

Ailill then greeted them fondly too. 'But what have you done with my son?' he asked. 'We have heard nothing since he left us to follow you.'

Aidan told them that Magdawna had travelled on to Datho's fort to return his people and property to him with due thanks.

'My son always knows how to behave correctly in every situation,' Maeve said smugly.

'Yes, *our* son is a true high noble.' Ailill was not about to let Maeve take all the credit for the good person Magdawna had become.

'Let us go to the palace,' Maeve said. 'When you have rested, come to my hall of judgement and tell me everything.'

An attendant picked up the silver bowl, and at once

staggered under its weight. He looked with disbelief at Brona. How could *she* have held this heavy burden high over her head for so long, he wondered. From that time on, rumours grew at Maeve's court about Brona's hidden power. 'Her strength is as the strength of ten', people would say whenever her name was mentioned.

Maeve led the company back into the fort and across its enclosure to her white palace. There the four children went to their own rooms. In each room a slave was heating bathwater by dropping hot stones into it. How often had the children dreamt of this moment during their long travels?

Their attendants were waiting to prepare them for a special reception banquet. Once again, Áilne plaited and braided Róisín's beautiful auburn hair and threaded it with beads and wove silver filaments and beads of pearl through Brona's. The attendant dressed them in long embroidered gowns, Brona's ornamented with clasps and brooches in silver filigree, and Róisín's with gold and amber ornaments. Over all this, Brona wore a cloak of forest green, and Róisín one of tawny orange that complemented her chestnut tresses.

In the same way, Rory and Aidan's servant Bress prepared them for the evening ahead. He tucked their short hair under jewelled headbands, which sat down on their foreheads like crowns. Their magnificent tunics were of white linen woven with gold. Over these Bress hung rich cloaks, Rory's of purple and Aidan's of deep red. They felt like princes.

When they were all ready, they went down to Maeve's great hall, where the queen was waiting for them. 'Come and sit around me,' Maeve said, indicating low stools placed in a semicircle in front of her. They sat at her feet to tell their tale. This time Aidan began, describing how he had decided on their path north and led them on their different journeys. From that point, others took over to relate various parts of the story. The queen did not interrupt until Brona reluctantly admitted that she had gone alone into Lú's fortress to bring out Datho's Bowl.

'Well?' Maeve asked, when Brona stopped. 'What happened? Why did guards not stop you? How did Lú not know that you had got inside his great hall?'

Brona could not break her promise to Pooka, yet she did not want to mislead Maeve or claim credit she did not deserve. She looked directly into Maeve's deep-violet eyes and spoke slowly: 'Majesty, you have always known that we came to you bringing strange secrets and hidden power. To reveal my secrets to you now would be to lose my power.'

Rory told the queen how Cruachan had given them the fiery chariot to bring back to Ardalba, where he thought Arch-druidess Scathach might be able to discover its secret.

'That wreck you were driving is the fiery chariot?' Maeve asked in amazement. 'Where is it now?'

'Your grooms took it, Majesty,' Rory replied. 'I'm sure it's safe.'

'Finish your tale,' the queen told them. 'Then I will send for Scathach. We do not need another fiery chariot, but who knows in what strange way its secret might help us.'

Róisín took up the story to tell about Sive, daughter of Ronan, and her role in events. Maeve was proud to hear how Magdawna had offered Ronan's gift of chariots to Falga, Eric and Penardun. 'They lost their own chariots because of evil Archeld,' she said. 'Now they are taking even better ones home with them. I am glad.'

Maeve had soon heard about everything that had happened. She at once sent a messenger to bring Scathach to her. When the druidess arrived, announced once more by attendants beating bodhráns, the queen explained that Ardalba was now in possession of the fiery chariot. 'Noble

Scathach, can you find out the secrets of the chariot if you study it?' she asked.

Scathach bowed low before her ruler. 'Majesty, allow the children to assist me, and I am certain that together we can succeed.' It was agreed that the four children would help Scathach examine the chariot the following day.

The time for feasting had arrived, and what a feast it was. They had all come through great dangers; this was the time to celebrate the victorious return of Róisín, Aidan, Brona and Rory from their expedition in the north.

After food and endless toasts of sweet mead, Maeve's bard took his harp to sing of the great events that had taken place. His song praised the four, turning them into heroes, and their recovery of Datho's Bowl into an epic event.

'We don't deserve all this praise,' Róisín whispered. 'Apart from Brona going into Carragdove by herself, we didn't do anything special.'

'Didn't we?' Aidan said. 'When have we ever done anything like that in Glenelk? *I* think it was pretty special.'

By the time the feast had ended, the tapers had burned low and the fire in the great brazier had smouldered to ash. The four children, too tired to talk any more, went to their rooms and slept soundly on soft beds.

\*

Next morning Scathach had the remains of the fiery chariot brought to her druid's hut, where she examined them from every angle. 'I see nothing at all unusual,' she said. 'Perhaps the children will see more than I do.'

When the four children arrived, Rory told the druidess about the hidden pieces of rose quartz Archeld had insisted Ronan should embed in the chariot walls, concealed under its silver panels. Scathach thought about this. 'They must be important,' she said. 'The first thing to do is to dismantle as much of the chariot as is necessary so that we can find this quartz. Will you do that for me, noble Rory?'

'Of course I will,' Rory said, 'but I will need a helper. Is it all right if Aidan gives me a hand? He's not a craftsman yet, but he's improving.' He gave Aidan a sly smile.

Scathach laughed. 'Not everyone is as gifted in woodwork and metalwork as you are,' she said. 'I'm sure Aidan will do anything you want him to. You'd better get started.'

For the rest of the day, Rory directed the dismantling of the chariot. Eventually the boys took off the silver panels without damaging them and began to look for rose quartz. It was not easy to find, as the pieces were tiny and had been set into small cavities in the wood, where they were almost invisible. By evening, they had found six pieces; they were fairly certain there were no more.

At the end of the day, Scathach came to find out how successful they had been. She held the tiny fragments of quartz in the palm of her hand. 'How could these produce blinding brightness?' she wondered aloud. The children gazed at the small pink particles in her palm and thought the same thing. 'We'll do some tests tomorrow,' the druidess told them. 'We're all too tired now.'

Later that evening, before the feasting began, there was a mighty noise outside the stockade, where lookouts saw Magdawna and cheered him as he rode home. Maeve and Ailill went out to welcome him, closely followed by the children. Soon he was inside the palace, where his attendants prepared him for a special welcoming banquet in his honour.

When everyone was assembled for the feast, Magdawna entered the hall. All the high nobles rose to honour him, their goblets raised. The prince had never looked so

magnificent. His tunic and cloak were the white that was Ardalba's distinguishing colour but were so heavily embroidered in gold and silver that it seemed he was dressed in precious metal. Around his neck he wore five strands of elaborate gold chain. Gold buckles fastened his tunic, and a mighty gold brooch held his cloak. The children had never seen him looking so regal.

The night flew by. It seemed over before it had properly begun. All four of them went at last to their rooms, where they fell asleep as soon as they lay down.

Next morning, when they had eaten their breakfast of oatmeal and honey, the children returned to Scathach's quarters. They found her poring over the quartz fragments in puzzlement. 'I have not found how to make these stones shine,' she said. 'The power must be in Archeld and not in the quartz.'

'Let me see them,' Brona asked. Scathach spread the small fragments out on the bench in front of Brona, who arranged them in a circle. Brona closed her eyes to gather her power and spoke loudly. 'By my own authority, I bid you shine,' she commanded.

Scathach was amazed to see the tiny pieces of rose quartz begin to glow brightly. When Brona opened her eyes, they stopped glowing. 'You are truly close to the Otherworld,' Scathach said. The arch-druidess now tried it herself. When she commanded the rose quartz pebbles, they shone for her also. 'Let us try together,' she suggested to Brona. They stood hand in hand, each directing their own inner power to the pebbles of quartz. This time the rose-coloured chips shone twice as brightly as they had before. 'I see now that I must focus my own power more intently,' Scathach said. 'With practice, I shall make the quartz shine as brightly for me as it did for Archeld.'

'Are they special stones, or would any rose quartz do?' Rory asked her.'

'That is a good point,' Scathach said. 'I have some rose quartz here, found in Ardalba. Let me try some of that.' She found the native stones and placed them on the bench. When she commanded them, they too shone.

When Scathach and the children told Maeve of their success, she called all the high nobles to a meeting of her Grand Council. Maeve wanted them to discuss how they thought the power to cause the stones to glow so brightly could best be used to help Ardalba. 'I want more from it than the ability to cheat in chariot races,' she declared.

All day long, nobles tried to come up with good ideas, but none of the ideas pleased the queen. Then Magdawna stood, seeking permission to speak. 'I am queen's champion,' he reminded them. 'I am the one who will first be called to single combat if Maeve should ever go to war or suffer attack from another ruler. My suggestion for using the shining power of the quartz is this. Implant a fragment of it in the outside surface of every warrior's shield, so that when it becomes activated it will blind enemies who oppose them in combat. Perhaps Archdruidess Scathach could instruct the warriors how to command the stone themselves, so that they would have this secret weapon wherever they were, without needing a druid to help them.' When Magdawna had sat down, all the members of the council clapped and cheered and stamped their feet. The idea was so simple, yet none of them had thought of it.

Maeve waited until the room grew quiet again. 'My son,' she said, 'I am proud of you.' She looked quickly across to where Ailill sat, and then amended her remark. 'Your father and I are *both* proud of you.' Clapping broke out again at this. 'It is fitting,' she declared, 'in fact it is *more* than fitting, when I go to war against Lú to fight him for his Brown Bull of Cooley, that the weapon with which I shall defeat him is one which he himself has devised.' There was more clapping and stamping of feet at this, until Maeve raised her hand for silence. 'We would not have this weapon now,' she said, 'without the bravery of Róisín, Brona, Aidan and Rory. Therefore I would honour them more than I have already done. Since they have twice defeated Lú, my enemy – once in Datho's race, and again in foiling his theft of Datho's Bowl – I can give them no better honour than to let them be known forever as Vanquishers of Foes, a title I now create for them.'

The queen sent for her Rod of Justice. She held it over Brona's head and declared, 'Brona, I name you Vanquisher of Foes.' Then she did the same for Rory, Aidan and Róisín. Such cheering and roaring and stamping and clapping followed that it was clear that all the high nobles were delighted with Maeve's decision. 'I wish their deeds to be recorded for all time by my annalist,' the queen continued, and sent for Ogma, the scribe.

Ogma, a small, bent man with a wrinkled face, arrived quickly, carrying a leaf-shaped piece of rough limestone which he had prepared by chiselling a straight line down the middle. Now it was ready for him to cut small notches on each side of the centre line. He knelt before the queen, hammer and chisel in hand.

As Maeve spoke, Ogma recorded. She had him list the children's names as the ones who had brought back the fiery chariot and its secret to Ardalba, a secret she would now use for the future defence of her territory. He was also to record Brona's skill in winning and then recapturing the silver trophy known as Datho's Bowl. Ogma chiselled the symbols on his stone tablet. He would later engrave it permanently on a standing stone, for all generations to read. The children thanked Maeve and Ogma, humbled by the thought that for the second time they had been entered in the official account of events in the Kingdom of Ardalba.

## 22

### BACK TO GLENELK

'What shall we do this afternoon?' Rory asked the others after the meeting. 'It's a lovely day.'

'I think we should go home to Glenelk,' Róisín said. 'If we stay another day, Maeve will find something else to keep us in Ardalba.'

This suggestion made the others stop and think. Sometimes they almost forgot that they did not really belong in Ardalba at all. 'You're right,' Aidan said. 'We've been here for ages this time. What do you think, Brona?'

'We've brought everything to a good conclusion for Maeve. I think we should leave,' she said. 'But first we should say goodbye to Pooka.'

'Let's do that now,' Rory suggested. 'Let's go to Boar Head Mountain. Then we can go to our cave straight from there.'

The four set out as they had done so often to go to Pooka's mountain. They climbed up beyond the waterfall and through the trees that grew thickly on the steep slopes. 'This is where we first met him,' Róisín said. 'Let's stay here and wait.'

'Let's call him,' Brona suggested. 'He's answered our call before.'

They called softly, 'Pooka! Pooka!' Brona closed her eyes

154

as she called, and summoned him in her mind: *Pooka, we're leaving. Come and talk to us.*

Suddenly he was there in front of them, plumes of fire blowing gently from his nostrils. His black coat shone and his creamy tail swished to and fro. They were speechless for a moment, then they rushed over to stroke his massive head and let him nuzzle their hands. 'We're going home, Pooka,' Róisín said. 'We want to thank you for helping us, and we want to say goodbye.'

They heard his husky voice in their ears. 'Goodbye,' he said softly. 'I can help you no more once you have left this time and place.'

Each of them stood in front of the horse to put their arms around his neck and to stroke his forehead, which felt like velvet. He rested his head on the shoulders of each of them in turn for a few seconds, and whispered to them: 'Goodbye. You can always find me here on Boar Head Mountain.'

Brona was the last to reach him. She stayed for a moment after the others had begun their journey back down the mountain. 'Thank you for making me invisible at Carragdove,' she said. 'Because you asked me not to, I have told no one of your help.'

'I helped you because you stand close to the Otherworld,' Pooka said. 'I could not help other people in the same way, but if you had told of my help, then they might have expected me to.'

'I understand,' Brona said, 'and now I must leave you, at least for a time. I'll miss you.'

Pooka once more blew fire from his nostrils towards her, and again she had the feeling she had had when Pooka had helped her to win the chariot race and later to carry the heavy silver bowl. 'Goodbye,' Pooka breathed. Then he turned and galloped up the mountain. She stood until he was out of sight before turning back to follow the others.

When she had caught up with them, they were discussing their clothes. 'Last time we wore slave clothes back through the tunnel,' Róisín said. 'Will what we have on now do instead?'

'Of course it will,' Aidan assured her. 'We wore slave clothes to escape from Maeve secretly. There was no other reason for them.'

Rory looked down at his white tunic and warm brown cloak. 'So long as we're not wearing fancy banquet clothes and all the gold stuff, we'll be all right,' he said. 'We wouldn't want to leave valuables like that hidden in the cave in Glenelk, would we?'

'What about Maeve?' Brona asked. 'Aren't we going to say anything to her?'

'What's the point?' Róisín asked. 'If we did, she wouldn't agree to our going. But if we go anyway without telling her, she won't even miss us. Time here will stand still until we come back, and she'll never know that we left.'

By now they were back down the mountain and could see Maeve's white palace in front of them, partly hidden by the wooden stockade surrounding the fort. People were going about their normal business. The four walked around the fort and headed across the valley towards the entrance to the cave. They peered around bushes until they found the way in, then took a last look back at Ardalba and stepped into the gloom of the cave. No one had missed them; no one was following.

They walked on through the darkness, feeling their way along by the wall. In no time at all they were back in the inner cave, where they had left their ordinary clothes. In what little light there was, they changed back into their jeans and jackets, leaving their Ardalba outfits rolled into small bundles in the darkest corner of the cave.

'No one touched them the last time,' Róisín said, 'so I suppose they'll be safe there this time too.'

When they were all ready, they followed Aidan into the outer cave, and from there into the Valley of Rocks, which was still bathed in sunshine. They found a warm place where they could sit in a circle, and thought back over their adventures.

'Do you know what?' Róisín said. 'People think the Celts used chariots, but no one has ever found remains of chariots in Ireland. We are the only people in the country who know for certain that they *did* use them.'

'Tell you what,' Rory said, to prove that there were things *he* knew about. 'Do any of you know that the writing Ogma chipped into the stone was invented by him? It's called Ogham, and you can see it on standing stones even today.' Rory was delighted to be able to have some information to match Róisín's.

'How do you know that?' Aidan demanded, never sure about things Rory told him.

'I know because I saw some when I was on holiday in Cork,' Rory said. 'There was this standing stone sticking up in a field, and when you looked at it you could see lots of little notches chipped out at the corners. People couldn't understand for ages what they meant.'

'They mustn't have known about ordinary writing,' Brona said. 'It would be easier than chipping stone.'

'I wonder whether the stones that we saw Ogma chipping our names onto are around here anywhere,' Róisín said. 'If anyone found them today, they could read about us and what we did in Ardalba.'

The children were quiet for a while, thinking about that.

Then they all stood up together. 'I could do with some real food,' Rory said.

'Yes, let's go home,' Brona said. She sounded a bit sad, because at home she was no longer near the Otherworld. Perhaps it didn't exist in Glenelk, she thought.

'Come on,' Aidan said. 'We had an exciting time in Ardalba, and we can always go back there, but here is where we belong.'

'And we're still high nobles,' Róisín reminded them.

The four set off for Glenelk, glad to see that their school and St Olaf's Church were still standing where they had been before. When they passed the church, its clock struck six.

'It'll be nice to be with our parents again,' Róisín said.

'Yes it will,' Aidan agreed. 'Come on! I'll race everyone to the Town Hall.'

They all ran laughing down the road, knowing that none of them would catch up with Aidan, the fastest runner in the school.